PR

She's having his baby—
but she longs for his love...

She's been seduced in the bedroom, and now
she's pregnant by the man of her dreams.
But will she ever have the one thing she wants
more than anything—his love?

Don't miss any of the stories in this month's
collection!

Price of Passion
Susan Napier

All Night with the Boss
Natalie Anderson

Bedded by a Playboy
Heidi Rice

The Pregnancy Ultimatum
Kate Hardy

We'd love to hear what you think about
any of these books. Email us at
Presents@hmb.co.uk and find out more
information at www.iheartpresents.com

Possibly the only librarian who got told off for talking too much, **NATALIE ANDERSON** decided writing books might be more fun than shelving them—and boy, it is that! Especially writing romance—it's the realization of a lifetime dream kick-started by many an afternoon spent devouring Grandma's romance novels. She lives in New Zealand with her husband and four gorgeous-but-exhausting children. Swing by her Web site anytime—she'd love to hear from you at www.natalie-anderson.com.

ALL NIGHT WITH THE BOSS

NATALIE ANDERSON

PREGNANT MISTRESSES

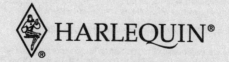

TORONTO • NEW YORK • LONDON
AMSTERDAM • PARIS • SYDNEY • HAMBURG
STOCKHOLM • ATHENS • TOKYO • MILAN • MADRID
PRAGUE • WARSAW • BUDAPEST • AUCKLAND

ISBN-13: 978-0-373-82062-7
ISBN-10:   0-373-82062-3

ALL NIGHT WITH THE BOSS

First North American Publication 2008.

ALL NIGHT
WITH THE BOSS

For Dave:
you said nothing is impossible and,
because I'm lucky enough
to have your support, you're right.

CHAPTER ONE

LISSA had just reached the railing when she heard the foot-steps behind her. Quickly turning, she sat on the bench in the shadows, hoping she couldn't be seen, just wanting five minutes' cool-down time.

She watched the approaching figure knowing full well she wasn't invisible and that he was heading right towards her. She didn't recognise him. She'd been at Franklin and Co. for five months now and knew everyone. Long legs wrapped in navy denim casually strode out with a grace that signalled a natural athlete. He was tall with dark hair. With the only light on the balcony being the thin streams escaping from the boardroom windows she couldn't see much more. She sighed, her heart sinking. Gina must have sent her friend Karl out to sit with her. Why was it that people thought set-ups were a good idea?

Unable to take her eyes off him she decided to ignore the tightening in her stomach and her promise to Gina to be 'open to possibilities'. Instead she would just get it over with. Tell it to him plain and then she could have some space again.

'Did Gina tell you I was out here?' She used her most decisive, not-to-be-messed with tone.

'No.' She caught a flash of white teeth as he smiled in the darkness. He sat down next to her with a companionable nod, setting his glass beside him. He'd positioned himself across from her, at right angles. His face was in shadow and he was close, too close. His presence radiated out, his legs near hers and she caught a faint citrus scent. Lemon, fresh and cool.

'Look, I'm sorry,' she began, trying for kind yet firm. 'I don't know what Gina told you, but I'm really not interested.'

'Oh.' He paused. 'Really?' He sounded quite surprised.

She took a deep breath and ploughed on, the words tumbling over each other in their rush to get out. 'It may seem hard to believe, what with everyone else so keen to get it on, but I'm really not looking for a bit of fun. I'm sure you are a great guy and all and you'll have no trouble finding someone else. Especially in there.' She emphasised by waving wildly at the window. 'After all, Gina says you're an amazing flirt.'

His sharp burst of laughter surprised her. Even more surprising was the way it resonated within her. It was deep, warm and dry.

'Does she? How nice of her.' He took a careful sip from his glass. 'But you know I don't think I want anybody else. Especially not "in there",' he mimicked her tone.

Her fingers tightened around the cool glass. She still felt hot and bothered and this interruption wasn't helping.

'Please yourself,' she said in resignation. 'But let's get one thing clear. It's not going to happen so we'll just chill, right?' She winced a little at her crabbiness, not intending to have spoken quite so baldly. She snatched a deep breath, trying to overcome it, but breathing properly seemed more tricky than usual when seated next to this guy.

'Suits me.' He was agreeable. 'Are you always this blunt?'

She frowned, her cheeks heating. 'Mmm. I'm sorry if you thought I was rude. I don't mean to be, but I don't want to have any misunderstandings.'

'OK.' He laughed, a shade too heartily for her liking.

She glanced at him, thinking he was pretty relaxed about being rejected from the outset. She could see a broad smile, an inviting smile. The kind of smile that made you want to smile right back and move closer to its warmth. She looked back to the windows and watched with cynical amusement as two consultants vied for Gina's attention. Lissa flicked a quick look sideways at Karl again, wishing Gina had warned her he was the most physically attractive man on the planet and not just a super flirt.

'Now that we have that settled,' he said easily, 'why not tell me something about yourself?'

'What do you want to know?' Lissa asked. She'd just shot the guy down before he'd had a chance to start his engine, she didn't need to be totally rude.

'I don't know.' He stretched out a leg. It crossed in front of hers, a barrier between her and the door. 'How about where in Australia you come from?'

'The South Island of New Zealand,' she replied coolly, trying not to admire the long leg before her.

'Sorry,' he chuckled. Again the sound reverberated within her, tingling her insides. 'Will you ever forgive me?'

She shrugged off the mistake and the sensations. 'It's OK. I'm not one of those Kiwis who has a fit at being mistaken for an Aussie.' She took a sip of her drink. Despite the chilly air she was no closer to cooling down. She sat for a minute and then leaned towards him with a conspiratorial smile. 'To tell you the truth, I still can't tell the difference between Irish and Scottish accents.'

'How shocking.' He leaned in towards her and for a moment she wondered what he was going to do. What she was going to do. His proximity knocked her breathing. 'Which am I?'

'Um…' She was taken aback. He didn't sound much like either. He sounded pretty BBC to her. 'Scottish?'

He inclined his head and sat back. 'Indeed.'

She was feeling a little unnerved by the effect he was having on her. Unnerved by the fact she was sorry he'd just sat back. It was a dark, cool night and she felt warm and wobbly.

Gina popped into view again and Lissa watched as her face lit up as an unfamiliar man walked towards her.

'Oh, that must be the infamous Rory.'

Karl turned his head sharply and looked back through the window. 'Where?'

'With Gina.' Rory stood absorbed by Gina as she talked, her arms gesticulating wildly with her effervescent enthusiasm.

'Well,' said Lissa practically, 'I don't think she's going to have too much trouble, do you?'

'Trouble with what?' Karl looked back at Lissa.

'Rory,' she replied impatiently. 'She must have told you about him. He's just landed after a stint at the New York office. Come back as the youngest consultant ever to be promoted to partner. He's due to start tomorrow but there was a chance he might look in tonight. She's wearing the blue top specially.' She watched the couple for a while longer.

'I can't believe she thought she didn't stand a chance. I thought she hardly knew him. But he's obviously interested, don't you think? And so he should—she's amazing.'

'If you like that sort,' came the noncommittal response.

Lissa turned to him startled. 'She's a petite, natural blonde with amazing blue eyes and is totally vivacious.' She paused before adding with perverse pleasure, 'The only sort that doesn't like that doesn't like girls.'

'Ha!' he laughed softly. 'You think? I think many men might prefer tall, willowy types with big brown eyes and hair like golden honey.' Before she could stop him he reached out and touched a strand of her hair.

She stared, unable to move. Felt him gather a lock and tug

gently. Crazily she wanted him to run his hand the length of it. What he'd said finally registered and she bit back a smile. She tried to ignore the tantalising quality in his voice. He'd just, very flatteringly, described her.

'Willowy?' she asked, amused.

'Uh-huh. Very graceful.' His fingers twirled the strands of hair.

She took a deep breath. She was feeling no more comfortable. The whole purpose of her stroll onto the balcony was being sabotaged. He sure knew how to trot out a line. She pulled her hair free and decided to reiterate the position. 'I told you. You needn't bother.'

'It's no bother.'

He was watching her intently. She crossed her legs away from him and wiggled her foot. 'You know, he doesn't look anything like I imagined.'

'Who—Rory?'

'Hmm, I thought he'd be taller and more noticeable.' Her attention was wandering back to the presence beside her. He was definitely noticeable. She became acutely aware of his knee pressing against her leg. He must have moved nearer. It was warm and hard. She fidgeted and recrossed her legs.

'Why? How did she describe him to you?'

'Apparently, he's like God's gift.' Grateful for the diversion, she laughed and ticked the items off on her fingers. 'Tall, dark, handsome, great body, a tough boss, but one that they all admire.' She made a face. 'Sounds too good to be true doesn't he? This is the Gina version, of course. But the clincher is, and I'm quoting here, "when he looks at you, it's like you're the only person in the world. Amazing eyes."'

Her attention snapped to Karl beside her. She couldn't see his eyes at all clearly. The colour was impossible to tell in the shadow. Gina hadn't described them, she'd been more concerned with impressing on her that he'd be a lot of fun.

Lissa had the feeling he'd be more than fun and that was dangerous.

She switched back to her description of Rory. 'Apparently he's Mr Hard-To-Get. According to office legend, he has never had even the teeniest brush with any of the crew.'

'And that makes him hard to get?'

'Well, you know what this place is like, they're all over each other.' The flirty nature of the management consultancy where she was temping was legendary. It was staffed by about forty-five bright young things who were all athletic, artistic, intelligent and gorgeous—fun after hours was standard.

'It's not that bad, is it?'

'No, probably not.' She giggled. 'It just seems like it. They're all such shocking flirts. Office affairs never end well. Too complicated.' Complicated being an understatement—it was something she well knew, thanks to Grant. 'Then with Gina trying to set me up with you…' Her voice drifted.

'And what did she say about that?' He sounded very amused now.

She glanced at him and opted for the truth. 'That you were a gorgeous player who knows how to give a girl a good time.' Lissa felt a needle of guilt for so blithely repeating Gina's description but, sod it, Gina had meant it as a compliment and, frankly, the way things were going, she was absolutely right.

'And you're a girl who needs a good time?'

'Gina obviously thinks so,' she answered giving a rueful laugh. 'But actually no. When I want one, I'll find one myself, thanks all the same. She was concerned about you because you haven't been dating the last couple of months. She thought we'd be great for each other.'

'What, you haven't been dating either?'

She'd been thinking about it—trouble was the only people she met were co-workers and after Grant that was such a no-go. Precisely why Gina wanted to set her up with Karl for a farewell fling before she left the country. But Lissa was adamant the last thing she needed was to go out with a well-experienced flirt. Playing with fire and being the novice she was, it would only end in carnage. Slow and steady when someone safe appeared, that was the answer.

This guy wasn't safe. His knee was pressing against hers again and she could feel the warmth of him. She had the sudden desire to sit even closer to him, feel the length of his leg press against hers, not just his knee. That would be warm, she thought. Who was she kidding? It would be hot. He seemed to read her mind.

'Are you getting cold? We've been out here a while.'

She shook her head and answered quickly, 'I'm fine. Don't let me keep you, though, if you want to go back in,' she said sweetly, half hoping to get rid of him and half hoping he'd stay. He was amusing, and she had to admit she was quite enjoying the light flirtation. Nothing wrong with a little practice was there?

'No, I'm enjoying being out here. It's very refreshing. What is it you're drinking anyway?' He was looking at the contents of the glass dubiously.

'I'm not quite sure.' She studied the colour in the light. 'I think it might be an apple flavoured one.'

'An alcopop?'

She could hear the yeuch in his tone. 'It's nice. Sweet.'

'And it's also lethal if you drink it too fast. How many have you had?'

She sat straighter. 'It's my second.'

'And have you had dinner?'

She bristled. She turned to face him full on. Both her knees knocked against his. She ignored the thrill shooting up her thighs and the naughty urge to part them. She tipped her head back instead and challenged him. 'Are you leading up to an invitation or are you implying that I'm tipsy? Either way, the answer is no.'

He turned and leaned forward, looking right back at her, their faces inches apart. She sucked in her breath sharply; the light from the window was full on his face and for the first time she could see him properly. Peripherally she took in a strong jaw and straight nose, but it was his eyes that captured her attention. They were the most amazing emerald green. She stared—had never seen eyes so vivid. It was some time before she remembered to blink. They were the kind of eyes you could drown in, wanted to drown in. Brilliantly coloured, glittering and warm.

'Is that so?' he drawled, a smirk lifting the corner of his gorgeous mouth.

Fascinated, she watched as his lips curved upwards. They were full and inviting. She became aware that she had leaned towards him further and abruptly pulled herself up. She swung back to face the window. Hell, maybe she was a bit tipsy, she certainly was feeling a bit dizzy. Impossible. She hadn't had much to drink, so it must be lack of food.

'Yes it is,' she said with asperity. 'Don't think you can bully me into a date because of anything Gina said.'

He leaned forward on the seat, put his head in his hands and laughed helplessly.

'Oh, stop,' she said witheringly, watching him half in disgust, half in amusement. 'It wasn't that funny. You're trying too hard and, I've told you, there's no point.'

His laughter didn't stop and she began to wonder if there was something in the joke she was missing. He was finding her just a little too amusing. Enough. She was finally starting to feel quite cold and experiencing urges she needed to control. Urges to get closer to a guy she knew to be a player. Summoning her dignity, she stood.

'Are you going to go back in now and party?' He smiled, rising as well.

She realised then just how tall he was. She was no midget—in these heels she was almost six feet—yet he was a good couple of inches taller again. She had to look up to try to see into those fabulous eyes. Catching them looking at her so warmly, she immediately felt it best to look away, fast.

'Actually I think I'm going to go home.'

'Good idea,' he replied blandly.

She glanced back up at him. There was no condescension apparent in his face, but her hackles rose regardless. She needed to get away from here. Correction, right away from him. Had she underestimated Gina's ability to matchmake or what? This guy made her pulse beat.

'It was nice to meet you at last, Karl. Have a good night.' She nodded at him politely and, without thinking, held her hand out to shake his. As soon as he took it she realised her mistake. The physical contact sent a bolt of electricity surging up her arm straight to her heart, causing it to contract. His grip was firm. His skin warm and dry. Another tremor ran through her. His grasp tightened and they stood linked, staring at each other. Her pulse picked up and she felt the flicker of excitement in her belly. She saw the recognition in his face. She jerked her hand out of his instantly, muttered a barely intelligible 'goodbye', and headed for the door.

He watched her step away from him. Should he have told her? Probably, but the temptation had proved too hard to resist, was still too hard to resist. He glanced down the now empty corridor and slipped inside, not turning towards the party as he ought, but heading for the stairs as quickly as possible. An attack of the lusts. Hadn't had one this severe in…well, ever, he didn't think. Five minutes back on home soil and he was utterly tempted by a foreign Venus. He hit the ground floor unable to stop the smile as he stepped into the foyer.

Lissa breathed a sigh of relief. She couldn't do 'a little fun', as Gina had urged. Now was definitely a good time to escape. Deep in thought, she marched out of the lift and straight into the figure standing before it. Firm hands grasped her upper arms and her nose was sore from bumping against the hardness underneath the wool jumper, which was all she could see ahead of her.

'Oh, I'm so—' She stopped short as she looked up at whom she'd just cannoned into. Mr Green Eyes himself. She frowned deeply as she watched his smile widen with quite obvious amusement. 'What?' she asked, unable to stop the rude bite. He nettled her, put her off balance.

'I'm going to drive you home.' The easy note of authority irked her more.

'I don't think so.'

'Yes, I am.'

She frowned at him again. 'You can't drive; you've been drinking.'

'I've had one drink the whole evening and had food earlier. I'm fine to drive.'

Her frown morphed into a glower. 'My mother taught me not to get into cars with strangers.'

'I'm not a stranger. We've just spent the past half-hour getting to know each other.'

She thought about it for a moment, knowing she was weakening. Gina knew this guy well, and quite frankly, the idea of a ride home in a car was appealing. It would beat a crowded tube and ten minute walk at the other end. The strappy shoes weren't great long distance, not even medium distance.

Even more tempting was the idea of spending another ten

minutes in his company. Just a little more practice? Sharpen the flirt claws?

'Besides,' he continued to persuade—she knew he could sense success, 'you've made your lack of interest very clear. So you've nothing to fear.'

Have I? she thought. Damn. Seeing all of him properly for the first time in the lit foyer, she realised her instincts had been right. He was one sexy animal. She stood staring up at him, her mind refusing to compute as quickly as usual. All she could seem to focus on were those fabulous green eyes. She saw the amusement in them. Why it didn't bother her, she couldn't say. Rather she simply felt the urge to lean in and share the joke. He stepped closer and held her arms tighter. The contact broke through her clouded mind.

'Well, if you insist.' She attempted a laconic drawl.

'I do.'

She raised her eyebrows slightly and allowed herself to be guided back into the lift. She looked at him in query.

'There's a car park in the basement.'

Leaning back against the lift wall she avoided his gaze and speculated on his choice of car. It would definitely be fast and flashy. Hell, probably a convertible with heated leather seats.

He took her arm again as they exited the lift and steered her through the line-up of closely parked cars. She tried to ignore the sensations that his thumb and every one of those fingers were causing. They were needles of electricity, points of awareness pressing into her. She pulled her lips into her mouth and pressed on them hard.

She wasn't at all prepared for the slightly dented, giant maroon people carrier that he stopped beside. The seven-seater was obviously used to being full. There was the unmistakable smell of infants. An assortment of papers and candy wrappers was scattered on the floor and two of the rear seats were fitted with child restraints.

'Are we expecting anyone else?' she asked blandly.

'No,' came the equally bland response. She sat down and made to fasten her seat belt. Suddenly she stopped. Reaching underneath her, she pulled out a half-eaten pack of now very squashed raisins. Wordlessly she passed them to him.

'Oh, good,' he said, taking them with a pleased smile. 'I was wondering where they went. Supper.'

She couldn't help but glance at his left hand resting on the steering wheel. No ring, no obvious tan mark. Beautiful long fingers, neatly trimmed nails, a broad palm. She shivered and looked away. This was Karl wasn't it? The incorrigible flirt? Confirmed bachelor and man about town? This definitely didn't go with the image.

'It's my sister's car.' He finally offered an explanation. 'Mine wasn't available and so I borrowed hers. She has three kids. Messy ones.'

'Oh, nice for you.' She clicked her seat belt into place. 'So what kind of car do you usually drive, then?'

'What do you think?'

'Oh, I dunno. Some sporty thing. Fast, flash, something to wow the ladies.'

'I don't need to rely on a car to wow the ladies,' he said suavely.

'Oh, really?' She couldn't help laughing.

He shook his head at her, laughter lighting his eyes so they glowed, burning into her.

'So what?' she asked with tart humour. 'You just rely on your dashing good looks, amazing physique, rapier-like wit and charm?'

'D, all of the above.' He nodded seriously.

She bet he did. He had all of those attributes in abundance.

'Now, where are we going?'

She looked at him in confusion before realising they'd been sitting there a couple of minutes and he hadn't started the engine yet.

'Oh, St Katharine's Dock, Tower Hill.'

He looked at her with raised brows, turning the key in the ignition. 'I thought it would have been Earl's Court or Shepherds Bush. Isn't that where all you Kiwis and Aussies hang out?'

'Maybe.' She shrugged. 'I'm not into that scene.'

'Avoiding your country folk?' He edged the car out of the garage and into the line of traffic.

'No, but if I wanted to spend all my time going to antipodean pubs and hanging out with other New Zealanders I wouldn't have bothered leaving New Zealand in the first place.'

'Running away from something?'

'Running to something,' she corrected. 'Don't get me wrong, it's not that I don't like New Zealand, I love it, but I wanted to travel and experience London. It's such a great city.' She sighed happily.

'So you chose St Katharine's Dock?' They were driving along Embankment, and she couldn't help but enjoy the famous buildings as they slid past.

'Yeah.' She smiled. 'Not in one of those amazing waterside warehouse conversions though. There's an old estate just at the back of them. I have a teeny flat there. It's fantastic. You know, I walk past the Tower of London every day on my way to work and every time it just hits me: I'm in London! It's awesome.'

'It's really such a dream for you?'

'Oh, yeah. It's all those years of having to watch *Coronation Street*, I guess.'

'*Coronation Street*?' he echoed blankly. 'But that's Manchester!'

She giggled. 'Oh, *Eastenders*, then, whatever. All those

royal variety shows; we get them all, you know.' She turned
to look at him, wanting him to understand. 'It's so great here.
Anything you want to do you can do in London, everything
is here for the taking.' She gestured widely with her hands.

He looked at her and smiled straight back into her eyes, and
her breath caught, he had the most magnificent smile. Her
heartbeat accelerated alarmingly. She looked away, hurriedly
dampening the attraction raging in her.

'You sound like such a tourist, all that fresh-eyed enthusiasm,' he teased.

'What's wrong with that? It's good to have some passion.'
Flirt alert—she willed serenity to return to her mind and body.

'I agree. Are you as enthusiastic and passionate in other
areas of life?'

She threw him a mock-evil look knowing she'd asked for
that one. He grinned wickedly back at her.

She took a breath and played safe. 'I love walking past the
Tower each day, laughing at those other tourists getting ripped
off by the most expensive ice-cream man in the world!'

'Really?' He laughed.

She nodded. 'He has his van there by Dead Man's Hole.
The most shocking prices.'

'Hmm. But I bet he's not as expensive as the gelato man
by Ponte Vecchio in Florence.'

'Really? In Florence?' She sighed longingly. 'I didn't make
it there. I'd love to go.'

'It's beautiful. I'll take you.'

She raised a brow at him, hoping her façade was as cool
as her insides were hot. 'Will you, now?'

He nodded. 'You have to see Botticelli's Venus. You're a
dead ringer.'

There was a silence as she absorbed the compliment.
Botticelli's masterpiece hung in the Uffizi gallery. His depic-

tion of Venus was one of the world's most famous works of art. Generation after generation admired the beauty of her. Lissa was amused, 'incorrigible flirt' was definitely the way to describe this guy. The trouble was, she couldn't help but enjoy it.

'Oh, you are good,' she cooed.

He smiled back winningly. 'And is it working?'

Yes, she thought, most definitely. 'That's for me to know…' she began.

'And for me to find out,' he finished. 'Good.'

What did 'good' mean? Had she just issued the man a challenge?

They entered St Katharine's Dock and she directed him to her building. Part of her wanted to escape the car as quickly as possible, but a good half of her wanted to stay and explore 'possibilities' with Karl as Gina had suggested. Then again, he might not really be interested. He might just have been working on his 'rapier-like wit and charm'. She glanced at him and realised he was watching her, an amused smile flitting around the corners of his mouth.

She stiffened. Had her internal debate been written all over her face? Probably. She strove for dignity. 'Thanks very much for the ride home. It was very kind of you.'

'No problem. It was a pleasure.' He replied equally formally.

She undid the seat belt and opened the door, sliding out. Surprised, she saw he was mirroring her actions. He walked round to stand beside her.

'I thought I'd see you to your door,' he explained. 'I wasn't sure you could manage the stairs.'

She looked up at him, amazed. 'Of course I can. What do you think I am? Blind drunk?' Far from it, but she had to admit she did feel wobbly. Food, she reasoned. It was lack of food, not the proximity of the male in front of her.

'No, but maybe a little tired.' He laughed. It had the effect she was getting used to, making her meltingly vibrant. 'Aren't you?'

He was standing too close. She stood looking up at him, mesmerised as he came even closer.

'If you're quite sure you can manage, I'll leave you,' he said softly, still coming nearer.

'Uh-huh,' she replied, rooted to the spot. He was gorgeous. Tall, sexy, fun. She knew she should be marching straight up those stairs pronto, but she just couldn't seem to get her legs to work. She stared up at him spellbound.

He reached out and stroked her hair gently. 'Bye, beautiful,' he whispered. Then he slid his hand down to the back of her neck in a loose caress, bent his head and kissed her.

It was the merest touch, light as a feather. Soft, warm, sweet, his lips just grazed hers. Then he broke the contact. She drew a sharp breath, her senses kick started and just when she knew she wanted more he returned, stealing the initiative, with full pressure. Firm, insistent, delightful. His hand cradled the back of her neck, his thumb stroking gently. Small sweeps upwards that had her softening, leaning closer, wanting yet more. She felt the weight and warmth of his other hand as it came to rest on her lower back. She wanted to touch him. She couldn't help but kiss him back. Her mind wouldn't focus on the fact that this was a really bad idea. It was only interested in the sensations he was stirring.

The hands she had raised in a defensive gesture didn't push him away. Instead they slid up his chest, feeling the soft wool jumper and the hard muscle it sheathed, and reached around his neck. It was warm and smooth. He stepped closer so their bodies touched, length to length. The impact was so pleasurable she gasped. Opening her mouth to his she tasted him. Their tongues met and entwined and her mind blanked out completely. Her body reacted instinctively, her breasts tightening, tensing, her mouth softening, ripening, wanting him in. Eyes closed, she breathed in the faint lemony scent that was so heady and delicious. Her fingers curled into his hair and she held him to her. Her toes curled in her sandals and tension swelled. The magnetism, their hold, was unbreakable. The simple goodnight kiss became something much, much more.

His hands stroked down her back, pressing her against him. She loved the feel of his hard body against hers, all of it. She melted, her curves fitting to him. She worked her fingers through his hair and pressed herself against him as much as he did against her. Breathless, she trembled and gloried as he tightened his grip in answer. She felt his hands slide down over her skirt, holding her hips to his. Her bones liquefied and an almost intolerable heat washed through her. His hands stroked lower down the length of her skirt, slid under and back up her legs. His fingers encountered the top of her lace stockings and traced over and onto bare flesh. Skin on skin, incandescent. She heard him groan against her mouth as she moved her hips restlessly.

It was the alarm bell she needed. God, what was she doing? She tore her mouth from his and stepped back. Shocked and embarrassed about the ferocity of the kiss, she was unable to meet his eyes. Instead she looked across at the block of flats, begging her body to calm. She feared that if she looked at him again she would throw herself back into his arms.

He had let her pull back and said nothing, but she was aware of his deepened breathing. Her body clamoured for more of that kind of action. That had not been some chaste farewell kiss, it had been the ignition to a passion that would have led to an explosive encounter with only one conclusion. She was not about to have a one-night stand with her best mate's friend. Especially when she knew him to be a flirt, a good-time guy. No wonder he was such a phenomenal kisser. He had plenty of experience. Attraction turned to anger, more with herself than at him. He was just doing what came natural; her response hadn't been. No way could the depth of feeling from that one kiss be natural.

'Goodnight,' she muttered. She walked away from him, fossicking in her bag for her key as she climbed the stairs. It was not until she was up on the little balcony on her floor that she dared look down at him. He was leaning against the car, one leg resting over the other, his arms crossed, staring up at her. Although it was hard to tell in the gloomy light from the streetlamp nearby, she was sure he was grinning. He waved up at her casually. Agitated, she turned and miraculously got the key in the lock first time. She opened the door and slammed it behind her, not chancing another look back.

Five minutes later she tilted her head to let the hot water beat down on her neck as she showered. She couldn't help but smile as his teasing lilt rang in her ears, couldn't help the inner glow as she remembered his smile, couldn't suppress the shiver as she relived that kiss.

Oh, boy.

Big mistake.

Temptation whispered in her ear. It was Karl. Gina's friend. She didn't work with him—it wouldn't be an office affair. What harm could come from a fling? It had been so long. Basic, carnal lust, of lethal magnitude. Touch an element that hot and you were bound to get burns. Third degree.

And she was leaving in two months' time. It would be madness to embark on something she sensed could be so strong when who knew how out of control things could get? No fling—not with him. Slow and steady with someone safe, remember? That was what she wanted.

CHAPTER TWO

GRUMPY from lack of sleep she popped a fizzy vitamin tab into a glass of water and knocked it back. She'd have a more substantial breakfast later.

'What happened to you last night?' Gina was sitting at her desk munching through a bowl of cereal, her computer switched on and already running through a complicated-looking search request.

Lissa looked at her in surprise. She was almost certain Gina would have spoken to Karl already. She decided to play for time. 'I wasn't really up to it. I sat outside for a while and then went home early. What about you?'

Gina eyed her speculatively. 'I'm sure there's more to it, you have a guilty look.'

Lissa felt her face flush but dampened down the feelings of embarrassment and focussed on Gina's own exploits. 'Well what about you? You must be feeling pretty happy this morning!'

'Why? Complete opposite, actually.'

'Why? It looked like things were going great! You guys looked totally hot for each other!'

Gina looked at her, perplexed. 'What are you talking about?'

'You and Rory,' Lissa said impatiently. 'He couldn't take his eyes off you.'

'Rory? He wasn't even there!'

Lissa's head snapped back. 'Yes, he was. I saw him talking to you; tall, dark, wearing a black leather coat.'

'Oh!' Gina started to laugh. 'That wasn't Rory, that was Karl.'

The earth tilted under Lissa's feet. 'Karl? The guy you were talking to? That was Karl?'

'Of course!'

'Oh, God,' Lissa breathed, her heart pounding. 'Then who was—' She broke off.

Gina watched her curiously. 'Who was…?'

Voices came louder along the corridor and Gina hurriedly put her bowl of cereal behind a stack of books on the corner of her desk. Lissa reached behind her to put another magazine on the pile to hide it effectively. They stood side by side as a group of consultants came in with Hugo, the head researcher.

'Gina, Lissa,' he began with an evil smile, 'we have some fresh blood for you. Gina, you must remember Rory—he's back from the New York office.'

Lissa saw Gina's sharp glance at Hugo. Hugo was by no means deaf and was fully aware of the numerous times Gina had discussed The Return with Lissa. There wasn't much Hugo didn't know. Oh, the joys of working in an open-plan environment.

Then she looked at the tall man stepping out from behind Hugo. Oh. My. God. Tall, devastatingly handsome in a suit and smiling straight at her was 'Karl' of the previous evening. He was Rory? Those fabulously unforgettable green eyes were now honed in on her with wicked laughter lurking in their glowing depths. She stared, unable to think anything but that he was even more handsome first thing in the morning freshly shaved and suited.

Hugo was going on to introduce the other men but Lissa didn't catch any of their names. Her legs were as wobbly as a newborn lamb's. Finally she dragged her gaze away from him and tried to start breathing again. She smiled in automaton fashion at the others and simply wanted the ground to open up and swallow her. Snatches of conversation came back to her: *'God's gift'*, *'when he looks at you...'* Oh, my God, what had she said?

She became aware that they were moving off to inspect the database terminals in the main library area. Lissa stood right where she was, looking down at Gina's swivel chair.

'I should have told you.'

She looked up, horrified to see that Rory had not moved away with the others, but instead had moved closer to her, too close. He was still smiling and she watched as he looked over her with a glint of appreciation. A trace of anger flicked through her, raising her temperature even higher. She eye-balled him, refusing to acknowledge the flicker of attraction that also sky-rocketed unbidden.

'Yes, you should have,' she whispered.

Annoyingly his smile widened further. Charming, cajoling, overwhelmingly attractive. 'I'm sorry; it was irresistible.'

'It was unforgivable. You must have known I'd mistaken you for someone else.'

'Mmm.' He looked back at the group of consultants before asking with seemingly genuine concern, 'Have you got a headache this morning?'

'Certainly not.' Irritation caused her to raise her voice louder than she had intended. She looked across to the others and saw Gina was watching, round-eyed.

'You'd better go and join the others.' Her body chose that exact moment to reminisce on how well his frame had melded to hers. She felt the fire in her cheeks and swallowed hard. She began to realise the full implication of his true identity. The situation had taken a total dive. He worked here. She couldn't avoid him and she really needed to. She couldn't be into this guy, not if he worked here, not at all.

'I've only been away six months,' he replied. 'I think I can still find my way round the library OK.'

'Well, I have work to be getting on with.' Too mortified to be able to see even the smallest funny side.

'Please don't let me stop you.'

Miraculously she gained the use of her legs and marched over to her desk and sat down, hating the fact that he was there to see that she hadn't even turned her computer on yet.

He leaned nearer. She felt his closeness with every cell. It was almost a pain. Her body yearned for him to reach out and touch her.

'Bye, beautiful,' he whispered.

Flushed with anger, embarrassment and desire, she stared at her computer screen as she felt him rise and walk away. She could just picture his grin.

Rory only just managed to stop himself running his fingers through her hair by jamming his hands into his pockets and striding back to where Gina and the new consultants stood. He couldn't help the grin on his face, though, and knew it was wholly because of wicked thoughts, not excitement about new computer systems.

First day as partner and all he'd been able to think about was getting to the information centre as soon as possible to see if she really was there; if she was real.

Well, now he knew. Definitely real. Definitely gorgeous and definitely ought to be off limits. He yanked his mind back from its determined wanderings into extremely dangerous territory and thanked God she'd been wearing trousers. He rolled a pen between his fingers, trying to stop the memory of the sensation when he'd crossed from stockings onto bare skin.

He was on the fast track, just made a partner and had worked damn hard to get there. The last thing he needed was distracting by a lust-on-legs temp.

Then again, just because he had career ambitions didn't mean he had to live like a monk. It wasn't as if he were thinking anything serious here. Marriage and kids were in the long-term plan, but short-term? Hey, he was a man, after all.

Office affairs did get complicated, though. He'd seen it a million times. Never got involved himself as a result—part of his unwritten code. Work was for work, play came after.

But she was a temp—and a New Zealander at that. She'd be onto another temp job or another country in no time. Perfect match for a full-throttle, fast-burning fling.

A partner and a temp, though? Dodgy waters.

He smiled his thanks at Gina—absolutely none the wiser about any of the new databases she'd just run through for him.

'Tell. All. Now.'

One look at Gina's face and Lissa knew she couldn't fudge it. 'I thought he was Karl.'

'What?'

'Rory. I thought he was Karl. At the party.'

'At the party?' Gina echoed. 'Rory was there?'

'On the balcony.'

'You didn't come in?'

'I went home early. He gave me a lift.'

'O-K…' Gina stood, positively agog. 'So what happened?'

Lissa felt the heat in her cheeks again. She fussed with her mouse. 'I, er, told him I wasn't interested.'

'What?'

'I thought he was Karl and that you'd set him up to come flirt with me, so I told him I wasn't interested.'

Gina started to laugh. 'And a fat lot of notice he took of that!

I knew it would happen like that. Man, that's why I wanted Karl to keep you out of the way so I could have just one chance with Rory before he saw you.'

'What?' Now it was Lissa who couldn't keep up.

Gina sighed. 'Look, babe, I've known Rory for ages and he's never shown a flicker of interest in me or any other girl here. We all drool over him and he's just Mr Charming to everyone. I was hoping that maybe when he got back he'd see me in a new light. I wanted Karl to eliminate you from the scene.'

'Eliminate me?'

Gina rolled her eyes. 'Look at you. Tall, legs that go for ever, curves in the right places. Long, beautiful hair. Frank and funny. You're a bloke magnet. Look how many of the guys have tried to chat you up and yet you won't go out with any of them. You're the female equivalent of Rory. Gorgeous and unattainable. It was obvious you two would hit it off.'

'Unattainable?'

'Yes, and even if you aren't that's the vibe you give off.' Gina looked at her slyly. 'But I just saw the way he was looking at you and, let me tell you, I've never seen him look that way at anyone before. And I've never seen you look flustered before. And you definitely look flustered.'

Lissa put her elbows on the desk in front of her and rubbed her temples.

Unattainable? She hadn't exactly been unattainable last night. She'd been easy, almost. Until now her desire to be unavailable in the office had succeeded. But Rory had shown that shield to be worthless. He'd shattered the illusion just by looking at her. This couldn't be happening.

He wasn't Karl the flirt. She needed to snap out of it and fast. He was a partner—one of the bosses. Been there, done that, and complicated wasn't the word. She'd had one of the best graduate jobs on the market and had ruined it by having an affair with her boss that had turned really nasty.

She forced herself to concentrate, and like the others worked through lunch. Come two o'clock everyone was beginning to flag.

'Coffee?' Lissa asked. 'I'll go.' She was eager to stretch her legs.

Both Hugo and Gina looked up; Lissa grinned at the desperation on their faces. 'I'll be back in ten.'

She braced against the chilly wind and got there in record time. Glancing around as she entered, she froze on the spot as she saw Rory with two consultants sitting on the far side deep in conversation and coffee. As she looked across his head lifted and their eyes met. His were glittering green and she felt lanced by them, feeling the impact all the way through to her marrow. She told herself the heat in her cheeks was from the cold air not that hot look.

Placing the order quickly, she stood determinedly watching the barista do his stuff, trying not to listen to any sounds from the seated area behind her. Once she had the coffees she couldn't help a swift glance to the corner where he'd been sitting with the others. To her immense relief, the chairs now stood empty. Breathing out for the first time since she had entered the shop, she left it.

He was waiting by the door. She hadn't seen him and nearly dropped the coffee when he said straight into her ear, 'Let me carry those.' He had the tray from her before she'd computed what he'd said. She had no choice other than to turn and fall into step with him.

'Have you forgiven me?' He was watching her with those dancing eyes.

She said nothing.

'Are you going to talk to me?'

She stopped and growled at him. 'No and no.'

He smiled back at her. She looked away crossly and continued walking. Damn him for having such a gorgeous smile. It made it hard to stick to her resolve—impossible, in fact. 'You should have told me who you were.'

'Probably,' he admitted. 'But it was so much fun not to. It was very enlightening.'

'Gina will never forgive me. I hadn't told her everything.' The last part came out as a mumble and she was annoyed to feel the tell-tale heat rise in her cheeks.

'And I won't either,' he said easily. 'She never needs to know. Have dinner with me.'

The change in tack was a surprise. 'No.'

'Lunch?'

'No.'

'Coffee?'

'No.'

'Why not?'

'I don't do office affairs.'

'Neither do I.'

'Then why are you asking me out?'

'I'm willing to make an exception in your case. Anyway, who said anything about an affair?'

She bit back her smile. She'd walked into that one. She didn't blame him. Different time, different place, she might have been saying yes. But not in this universe. He was a workmate, more than that, he was one of the bosses. But she didn't want to drag up old issues and decided to deflect him with a different excuse. 'I don't like office gossip.'

He laughed aloud. 'What? You told me a fair bit last night.'

That one hurt because she knew it was true. She battled to bolster what she knew was a weak argument. 'I thought we were discussing a mutual colleague. I said nothing malicious.'

He stared at her thoughtfully. She bore the scrutiny as long as she could before glancing around, unable to take the heat and promise that glowed in his eyes. 'No one has to know,' he said softly.

For a moment she was tempted. Then reality slammed back. No, the best thing was to stay as far away from this man as possible. His gaze didn't leave her face.

'That would be impossible.'

'What others think is really that important?'

'Of course.' She frowned, knowing damn well it wasn't. Her mother had taught her to live life by her own rules, with dignity, without hurting others, and then no one had the right to judge. Of course, never date a workmate was one of the rules.

'That was no ordinary kiss, Lissa.'

She was glad she wasn't holding the coffee. She would certainly have dropped it then. He'd spoken so softly for a moment she wondered if she'd dreamt it. She didn't reply, couldn't. Damn, it would have been easier if he had been Karl, the flirt who she should definitely steer clear of. But he wasn't, he was Rory, an altogether different proposition, an altogether different danger and no less inappropriate.

They reached the building and she looked at him expectantly, wanting to take the tray from him. He shook his head and, clenching her teeth, she opened the door. Her heeled shoes clipped on the floor as she strode ahead to viciously press the button to summon the lift.

'You're very quiet today,' he commented. 'Funny, when you seemed to have so much to say last night.'

Oh, she had plenty to say all right, but she sincerely doubted her ability to say it without resorting to a number of four-letter words. But she'd been tactless enough last night. He was a partner, a boss.

They rode the lift in silence. Lissa tried to ignore his

nearness and failed miserably. She stole a glance at him and was flustered when she encountered him looking straight at her. She looked away again instantly and watched the floor numbers light up. Unable to stop herself seconds later, she glanced back. He was still watching her. He looked amused and a hint of satisfaction crossed his face. She seethed.

The doors opened on their floor and she burst out of the lift like a jack-in-the-box, desperate to get away from him.

'Don't forget your coffee!' His call brought her up sharp. Damn. She wheeled around. He was standing just in the foyer holding the tray out. Conscious of the receptionist not five feet away, she stalked back. She stopped a foot away from him and reached for the tray. He took a step nearer and placed it in her hands. His eyes not breaking from hers, he carefully put one hand on hers, then the other hand. Her skin sizzled and her fingers moved unsteadily. He curled his own fingers around hers, ensuring she held the tray securely. Thus they stood for a fraction too long. His hands on hers felt wonderful and she knew his full embrace would be equally dynamic. She pressed her lips together—how could this be? He was a man, like any other.

'Thank you.' Oh, was that eager whisper really hers?

'Bye, beautiful.' He gave her hands a little squeeze. Her heart and stomach contracted. He flashed her a heart-stopping smile before letting go and exiting through the staff door to the back offices.

Lissa stood immobile. He'd just taken her breath with him. She could still feel the pressure of his fingers on hers and his blazing smile was all she could see.

'Got a minute?' Hugo strode back into the information centre from a planning meeting. Gina and Lissa spun on their chairs to face him.

'We're reassigning researchers for the teams because of a

new project.' Hugo was straight to the point. 'Its very sensitive with major client confidentiality issues. Initially it's just
a two-week job and they want a dedicated researcher. Lissa,
you're it, starting Monday.'

Lissa stared at him.

'You can't work on other stuff at the same time because
you're going to be locked away in a meeting room. It's all very
top secret; the IT guys are setting it up now. It's a small team—
one partner, two consultants and you. You'll be expected to
prepare the final presentation and proposal. Typing and
overtime. You OK with that?'

Lissa nodded, fighting the bitter disappointment. She'd
spent most of the time working on a project for a company
based in Portugal. It was due to wrap shortly and as a reward
the team were going to be flown to Bilbao for a weekend and
a party at the Guggenheim. She'd been told she would be
included if still there at the end of the project. She'd been
looking forward to it so much. She hadn't had a chance to go
on her own travels there and now had run out of time. Her
return ticket to New Zealand was already booked.

'Go straight to Meeting Room Two on Monday,' Hugo continued. 'You can do the searches no problem and your computer
skills are excellent. The partner thought you'd be a great asset.'

She smiled, partly soothed by the compliment. 'Really?'

Hugo nodded. 'He hand-picked you. You'll be working
directly for Rory.'

After a predictably atrocious night's sleep she arrived fifteen
minutes early on Monday morning embarrassed to discover
she was the last to arrive.

'It's OK you're not late, Lissa.' Rory stood and walked
around the table towards her. 'We started earlier to generate
some work for you.'

She nodded, glancing at him. Their eyes met and held. She could see nothing in his other than professional politeness, but that didn't stop her pulse from accelerating as she registered how brilliantly green his irises were. As their gaze held his pupils dilated. Heat emanated and a rush of feeling rose from her belly to her breast. She snatched a breath and quickly resumed her contemplation of the computer set-up. 'I just want to check I have access to all the databases.' She tried to overcome her breathy tone and inject some professional assertiveness.

He nodded and gestured to the lone computer on the far side of the table. He followed her to her seat. 'We'll have breakfast and a debrief in fifteen, OK?'

She looked up at him, her insides flip-flopping all over the show. This time there was a knowing smile in his eyes. This was going to be much harder than she'd imagined. She stiffened and began checking the systems. She was acutely aware of him moving behind her to the other end of the table.

Sheesh. How was she going to cope with two weeks of him right by her side when she was so aware of his every move? When her whole body answered with such responsiveness to a simple look?

Ten minutes later she was satisfied IT had done a good job. Rory called for her to join them. She smiled warmly at Marnie, and then nodded coolly at James. He'd asked her out on a date months ago and had professed his devastation when she had refused. She'd soon learned that he made it his business to ask every temp worker out.

James filled the mugs from the coffee-pot while Rory outlined the project to Lissa. 'Our client wants to find a takeover or merger target asap in top secret.'

Almost immediately her thoughts went AWOL. It must have been the idea of merger. She watched him as he spoke, hoping her outward appearance reflected her concentration. Sure, she was focussed, but not on what was being said. His shoulders looked so darn broad. Fantastic for holding onto. She watched his hand as he tapped a pen on the notepad in front of him. Large and strong. She bet he didn't battle with the lids on jam jars the way she did. But she knew just how gentle they could be. Could imagine only too well how deliciously tormenting they might be on other parts of her body. She shuffled in her seat, a warm flush invading her nether regions.

James handed her a coffee. She took a deep sip, hoping the caffeine hit would clear her befuddled brain.

It worked. Momentarily.

'We'll be working round the clock for the next two weeks, but I'm sure that's not a problem for anybody?' Rory glanced at them.

Lissa was split. More hours with Rory, but her overtime rate was superb. Pots of money for a situation in which she had to fight the most powerful attraction she'd ever known.

He gestured towards the paper on the windows blocking the view to the corridor. 'The secret-squirrel stuff is for real. Save your social lives for lunch breaks, please.'

'What lunch breaks?' interjected James.

Rory grinned. 'I know, but it's only a fortnight and this is worth it. We do a good job and we could win a huge contract for the company. There's a lot riding on this and it could be good for all of us.'

Lissa wasn't at all sure how this could be good for her—locked away in a tiny room for hours on end with Rory? An intense, artificial atmosphere, the perfect breeding ground for an intense but artificial relationship. She had to be strong.

'So,' Rory continued. 'Lissa, we need you to research these companies and type up meeting notes, compile reports and the final presentation.'

'All that typing OK with you, Lissa?' Marnie asked.

Lissa smiled. 'It's fine. I'm just the temp,' she reassured.

'You're not "just" anything.' Rory interrupted. Lissa's mouth fell open. On the surface she felt embarrassed, but underneath the reaction was volcanic, the heat bubbling, desire swirling upwards. She looked down at the papers before her, willing someone to fill the pregnant silence. After a moment Rory quite calmly began outlining further details of the project.

She found it fascinating to watch him in action. The master of charm and attention, he seemed to enchant the others, made them want to do their best to please him. Slightly distanced, Lissa watched him weave this magic, witnessing their seduction. It totally irritated her.

When it came to giving Lissa instruction there was a flash of unholy enjoyment in his eyes that she couldn't miss. And a slight chink in her professionalism where she couldn't help but feel as if she wanted to do the exact opposite of what he requested.

Late on Tuesday afternoon only the two of them worked in the room. The silence sat heavy. Lissa tapped the keyboard and frowned at the screen, determined to pretend he wasn't there. As if.

Suddenly he stood. Well, she had to look then, didn't she? He stretched a little, the gesture emphasising his length. She knew she should look away, but it was impossible. He smiled at her—and the need to look away became imperative. Instead she couldn't help the small smile back.

'Come on, team-building.'

Her surprise must have been evident.

'Team-building,' he repeated, the dizzying smile widening. 'Some corporate R'n'R.'

She didn't trust him; that smile had turned a little wicked. 'Half the team isn't here.' She felt nervous about alone time with him outside the office. Memories of that hot embrace flooded her. Excitement trammelled through her, but she bolted it back down in her emotional cellar labelled 'do not enter'.

'They're coming once the meeting is over. Shouldn't be more than fifteen minutes. We'll only have time to get there and order the first round.'

It sounded harmless enough. They were meeting the others there. Besides, he was the boss. She didn't really have much choice. She nodded acquiescence and logged off her computer while he did the same. She got her jacket from the stand in the corner. She pulled it around her and secured the belt firmly, looking up in time to catch him watching her. A definitely sinful smile played on his lips.

Provoked, she deliberately pulled the ends of the belt a little tighter, pinching her waist, emphasising her curves, defiantly holding his gaze. Desire washed over his face, his eyes burning, the skin across his high cheekbones reddening, and she knew her own face mirrored his reaction. Her head tipped back a fraction, she felt the pulse in her lips, felt the longing for him to touch her bared neck. Sharply he turned to exit the room.

They walked to the lift in a silence that hummed with awareness. Mentally she berated herself for the flaunting gesture. Only the tiniest spark could cause an inflammation. Her lower belly and her breasts felt tight from the moment of blatant sexual encouragement. For an instant she'd let her control lapse and now she was paying for it. With every step she felt conscious of his nearness, knowing she wanted to be closer. Much closer. Bad, bad, bad.

Out on the street he surprised her by heading away from the usual company haunt. She tried to recover her equilibrium.

'We're not going to Jackson's?'

'Well, it wouldn't be much of a team-building exercise if we went to the local and had the whole company join us. This is just for us, Lissa.'

Just for us? Her pulse raced, beating off kilter again.

He kept walking, and talking. 'We're going to be working in close quarters for long hours. We need to be a tight unit. There isn't room for any issues or...' he paused '...distractions.'

Despite her flirt moment minutes ago, she had no intention of being a distraction. Nor was she going to be distracted. Uh-uh, no way.

'Marnie and James are competitive with each other. For the most part this is good, but I want the quality of our work to be the primary goal, not one-upmanship or point-scoring or—' he cleared his throat '...scoring at all, for that matter.'

'Scoring?' She stopped and stared at him.

His face was slightly reddened, but he met her look squarely with a gleaming one of his own. 'Lissa, I'll be honest with you. I'm attracted to you. Have been since the minute I laid eyes on you. That attraction only seems to grow the more I'm around you. But I cannot afford to screw up this project by spending my time chasing you when I should be working. Believe me, it's damn tempting. So I'm telling you now. I'm interested in you. If you feel the same, then let me know.'

Vaguely she sensed the movement of people passing them on the footpath, of buses and taxis slowly advancing along the street, but it was as if the world had subsided into fuzzy focus leaving only Rory before her, impacting on her with brilliant clarity.

Time held suspended as she saw him watching her as her brain ran through every ugly reason why she couldn't be honest with him or herself. She couldn't let anything happen, even though minutes ago she'd practically asked for it. He was her boss. Power plays couldn't help but enter the equation and she knew nothing about him. She couldn't risk it.

Finally she spoke, the raw sound embarrassing her. 'Rory, I can't. I just can't.'

He stepped an inch closer. 'Is that can't or won't, Lissa? I know you're single. I know you enjoyed kissing me.'

Denial was futile, her flush confirmed everything, and so silently she waited him out.

He blew out a deep breath. 'I'm taking it as a won't, Lissa. That's fine. So for now we concentrate on work. But once this project is wrapped then I think we revisit this conversation.'

The blood pounded through her body, her cheeks were still hot, her lips felt full. But she couldn't be a slave to her desire like this. She'd screwed up one good job already. She wasn't going to do that again.

He took her arm and gave her the benefit of a full-wattage Rory Baxter smile. 'Don't look so worried. It'll all work out just fine.'

He ushered her into the bar.

'You choose the table. I'll get the drinks—apple or cherry?'

She frowned at him.

'Alcopop? Which flavour?'

'Oh.' She felt the heat in her cheeks increase and the small smile popped out without her permission. 'Actually, I'll just have a lemonade, please.'

'Going straight tonight?'

Yes. Straight home. Alone. She nodded. She watched his authoritative stride to the bar. The barmaid leapt to attention, flicking her hair and offering a flirtatious smile.

Turning away before she acknowledged the sudden burst of irritation, Lissa chose the table under the brightest light in the middle of the room. No tiny dark corner to be secluded in, no hint of romance, of intimacy or intensity. She should have known it wouldn't work. Her brain had slipped a gear out of professional mode and into seduction. Her seduction. His approach on the street had surprised her, his unashamed acknowledgement of his attraction to her. But he had made it clear; work came first. This was good. What had he called it? A 'distraction'. That was all it would be. She needed to remember that. Men who had office affairs weren't thinking marriage and kids. More a bit of fun to liven up long hours at the office and more often than not they'd say anything to get it.

He came across to her, a drink in each hand, and selected the chair directly opposite her. No escape from his handsome face and penetrative eyes.

'You like working at Franklin?'

She had until recently. But her thoughts were interrupted by the harsh beep of Rory's cell phone. With an apologetic look he answered, yes-ing and no-ing for a few minutes. Flipping it shut, he looked at her with a twinkle in his eye that she was unable to interpret.

'That was James. They're held up in the meeting and want to rearrange.'

'Oh, OK.' Lissa knew more time alone with Rory couldn't be allowed. 'I should get on home.'

He gestured to her three-quarters-full glass and his own barely touched wine.

'Can't go wasting company money, Lissa. At least stay and finish your drink.'

It would be churlish not to, but danger signals beat strongly within her. She picked up the glass and had a long swig.

He chuckled. 'Do I make you that nervous?'

'Of course not.' She was more nervous of herself and her own silly weakness. She couldn't let herself be such a fool a second time, but the attraction to him threatened to overwhelm her.

'The indecision in your eyes just about kills me, Lissa.'

She looked down immediately. His soft-spoken bluntness slipped under her defences again. She bolted them down. He was direct at work as well. But was he honest? Or was it all just a line practised time and time again to perfection? Flash the green eyes, flatter the lady and raise curiosity to breaking-point. It would be so easy.

'I really should get home.'

'Should you?'

'Yes.' Definitely.

'Why don't we get something to eat before you do that?' She couldn't stop the sly smile. 'Nice try, Rory.'

'What?' He put up his hands, all mock innocence. Smiling, he lowered his voice. 'We will reschedule, Lissa.' The serious note struck a chord within her and she knew he wasn't refer-ring to team-building.

Declining his offer of a ride home, she escaped the bar and his breathtaking presence. Never one to miss the opportunity of seeing a few landmarks on the way, she took a bus. She only had weeks left to enjoy the sights. But as she sat in the window seat her eyes were unfocussed, and she was so intent on her own thoughts she missed her stop.

She had thought Grant was honest. Older, only by ten years, but infinitely more experienced. He'd known exactly how to pursue her in a way that didn't scare her off. He'd given her the works; attention, flowers, the romance she'd never experi-enced, never seen her mother enjoy, only knew of from the movies. That should have told her it had all been an act. She'd thought she loved him, that he'd loved her. That she was going to get the happy-ever-after her mother had missed out on.

Then she'd found out about Melissa. His fiancée. The sordid truth had become humiliatingly obvious. He'd never taken her to his apartment, had encouraged her to keep quiet about their relationship with other workers because he hadn't

wanted any hint of favouritism, they'd never gone out—he'd
come over to her place instead, cooking for her, flattering her
and all the while just using her.

Immediately she'd ended it. Or tried to. Only he'd turned
nasty. He'd made her work a living hell—denigrating her in
front of colleagues, giving her all the dogsbody jobs instead
of the work she was trained for and, occasionally, he had still
tried to touch her.

She could have taken a harassment case against him, but
she'd felt too bruised already, ashamed by the knowing looks
of her co-workers, the mortification of being the 'other
woman'—albeit innocently. What a fool.

So she'd packed her bags.

Now she'd met Rory. She knew nothing about him either
except, in a matter of only hours and days, he'd breached her
defences. She wanted him, plain and simple. Wanted to run
her hands over his body, wanted to feel him hard against her,
entwined with her. But she couldn't risk ruining another job
on her CV. The only way she could think to prevent it was to
freeze him out. Retreat behind a frosty veneer, not look at him,
not talk to him, only when necessary for work.

CHAPTER THREE

By Wednesday afternoon Lissa knew her plan was flawed. Rory's constant physical presence got on her nerves. For hours she held her body taut with awareness of his only a couple of feet away. When she looked up and away from her computer screen to rest her eyes, she couldn't help but glance at him. Invariably, she would find him watching her or he would look up as she watched him. She would look quickly away, biting on her lip. When that happened for about the fortieth time that day she was so mad with her weakness she rose to make an escape to the bathroom for two minutes. Just to get away from him, to stare in the mirror and remind herself exactly why she shouldn't be letting her lust for this guy affect her work. No distractions.

Walking back down the corridor on her way back, she was startled as her arm was wrenched and she was practically hauled into a meeting room two down from theirs. The door shut after her. She whirled round staring at Rory who now stood in front of the door, blocking her exit, his arms folded across his chest.

'What are you doing?' she whispered, struggling to regain her equilibrium. His nearness made it difficult for her to breathe, let alone concentrate on work. The tension between them crackled. The stance accentuated the breadth of his shoulders and she felt herself soften in response to his forceful masculinity. Her breathing became shallow and she tried desperately to stay focussed on the job. Think computer passwords, think phone numbers, think of anything but how sexy he looks. Suddenly his lips twisted and he laughed a little. It made it worse.

'Lissa, look, so we can't be lovers, I get that and I'm sorry if I embarrassed you, but can't we at least be friends?'

She looked at him with a sceptical frown. 'Do you really think that's possible?' When there was this much sexual chemistry simmering away barely below the surface, it felt as if it would take nothing for it to envelop and swamp them.

He looked across at her, his sensuous lips pressed together in a teasing half-smile. 'Oh, I think it's possible. I'm not going to have you on the desk at the first opportunity. I think I can keep my baser urges under control.' He lowered his voice and challenged, 'Why—can't you?'

She stared back at him in silence, her mind wanting to answer but her body having fixated on the idea of having him on the desk, the idea of having him full stop. She could picture him above her, easing her onto the hard wood, papers swishing to the floor. She caught her lip with her teeth and bit down, wanting the pressure to ease the pulsing. What she really wanted was another kiss.

His eyes narrowed as he regarded her. He stepped closer. Frustrated, she tore her eyes from his and looked down. He stepped still closer and took her chin with his fingers and tilted her face back up to his. 'Can't you?' he asked again, his voice rough. His fingers slid along the side of her jaw and down to her neck; his thumb gently rubbed over her lips, forcing her to free the lower one from her teeth. He rubbed his thumb back over, soothing it. It did nothing to stop the throbbing.

Their gazes locked again. She fought the urge to open her

mouth and suck his thumb in. Appalled with herself, she jerked away from his touch, backing away from him so the table was between them.

'Don't worry, I'm not into sexual harassment.' He glared at her, his hands on his hips. 'I promise I won't touch you again unless you ask.' He stuffed his hands in his pockets as if to emphasise it. 'If you keep freezing me out like you are today, then the rumour mill will swing into overdrive. And I know how desperate you are to avoid any sort of gossip.' Dripping with sarcasm.

She pressed on her lips again, deciding on her reply. 'Well, if you keep making comments like that one the other day, the tongues will already be wagging furiously.'

He raised his brows and looked mystified.

'The one about not being "just" a temp,' she explained crossly.

The brows shot down and a lazy smile stretched across his lips. 'Well, you're not "just" anything. You're just amazing.'

She looked away, attempting to diffuse the power that smile had over her. 'That's not helpful, Rory.'

'No, but at least it's honest.'

'Meaning?'

'Why not try being honest about why you're really refusing to go out with me?'

Too astute. There was more to it. She knew it and he knew it. She opted for denial.

'I have been honest. I don't like being talked about.'

He shook his head. 'No, I think there's more to it than that.'

'Like what?' Her heart banged even harder.

'I think you're scared.'

'Of what—you?' She tried for sarcastic but knew she'd failed. She sucked in a deep breath. He did frighten her, but she frightened herself more.

'No. Maybe. Yes.' His eyes bored into her. 'Scared of this

pull between us. It's damned strong, and don't pretend you don't know what I mean. I see it, Lissa. I see it in your eyes.'

Hell. She wondered if it would be OK to wear sunglasses in the office. She shrugged, deciding not to try to deny something that was so obvious to both of them. She knew he was right, about everything. This was Rory. Everyone got on with him, considered him an all-round good guy. The partner everyone wanted to work for. Her attempt at a reserved professional approach was too pointed, too icy to be unemotional. It would be misconstrued or, more likely, construed correctly. She needed to smarten up.

'It's new to me too,' he said softly.

She closed her eyes. She sensed he spoke honestly but it terrified her. She couldn't let her guard slip. She felt like a tiny metal pin attempting to resist a giant magnet. The laws of physics would deny her. But she knew she had to try. To jump into a fire this hot with her boss, when she had only weeks in the country? No. Not unless she wanted more heartbreak in her life. Which she didn't.

'I'm sorry. We'll try to be friends.' She looked around the room, wishing for another exit. 'Are we done?'

He looked at her sardonically. 'Not by a long shot.' But he stood aside and opened the door for her. She made her escape knowing he was only two steps behind.

Lissa rubbed at the pain in her temples. Last night she and Gina had spent a reasonably quiet couple of hours over a bottle of wine, and a plate of pasta in the corner of their favourite bar alternately discussing men—Gina's favourite topic—and travel opportunities—Lissa's. She'd needed to escape the office and her own thoughts and had hoped that a night out with Gina would help her achieve just that. She frowned as her computer clunked through processing her latest request. It hadn't worked. She utterly distracted; the cause of her headache was over six-feet in height and a force looming beside her, captivating her thoughts to the exclusion of all others. It was so frustrating. She sighed. Marnie noticed and guessed about her head.

'You've had your hair scraped back so tightly all week it's no wonder you have a headache.' Without further ado she came and stood beside Lissa, undid her clip and loosened her hair so it tumbled around her shoulders.

'Marnie!' Lissa protested.

'It's for your own good. Now…' Marnie sank her fingers into her hair and pressed on her scalp. Lissa had to admit it felt fantastic.

'I did a massage course to learn to relax.' Marnie explained. 'Is that OK?' she asked Lissa as her hands kneaded her skull right where the bands of pressure had been building.

'Oh, it feels great.' Lissa closed her eyes, the pain receding. 'That's amazing.'

'Don't I get one too?' James asked with a randy light in his eye impossible for anyone to ignore.

'No.' Marnie was basically rude.

'I can just watch,' he said, unabashed. 'I'm happy to watch.'

I bet you are. Lissa glanced at Rory to see what he was making of this bizarre situation. He was resting his jaw in his hand and watching too. A small smile flickered round his mouth.

Marnie finished. 'There you go. All better.'

'Can I have my clip back?'

'No, I'm confiscating it. You should wear your hair down. It looks nice.'

She didn't want it to look nice.

Rory looked thoughtful. 'Anyone got special plans for lunch?'

No one answered in the affirmative. Lissa assumed he wanted them to work through, again.

'Right, we're going out, then. Our missed teambuilding date.'

Lissa suppressed a sigh. Marnie and James were already grabbing their jackets and heading out the door, eager to escape the dungeon. Lissa sat fiddling with her mouse. Rory looked at her in inquiry.

'Do you need me?' she asked. 'I mean,' she continued hesitantly as she watched the dark look grow in his face 'you guys are the consultants. I'm just here to research and type.'

'I've told you already, Lissa—' his eyes glinted as he walked towards her '—you're not *just* anything. You're as much a part of this team as I am.' He stood right next to her and bent so they were eyeball to eyeball. 'You're coming even if I have to make you.'

He would make her come, all right. Of that she was certain. She sat stunned at her thoughts. Cursed that her mind should interpret his words in such a James-like fashion. She simply couldn't stop the wry twist to her lips. He saw it and his attention dropped to her mouth. Her lips softened and parted under the heat of his gaze. She heard his indrawn breath. She badly wanted to lick them they felt so dry and needy. Even more badly she wanted to taste his. Every fibre in her sprang to life as he inched tantalisingly closer.

Marnie popped her head back around the door. 'Coming?'

Rory's head lifted sharply. Their eyes met again and Lissa saw her own amusement reflected. He spun round. 'Just as soon as we can.'

Marnie glanced at Lissa. Lissa smothered her appreciative chuckle, met her gaze as coolly as she could and walked out the door after her.

They went to a small Italian restaurant not far from the office. James sat next to Lissa while Marnie and Rory were across from them. It was not a large table and as they sat Lissa felt

Rory's knee press against hers. Hurriedly she moved back a little, studiously perusing the menu and avoiding the smile she knew would be on his face.

They ordered and ate and Lissa sat quietly letting the leisurely work chat wash over her. The food was delicious and she was starving. The main course passed by in a flash. She smiled at the waiter hovering near, nodding for him to hand her the dessert menu. She licked her lips as she mentally debated between the white chocolate and raspberry torte and the lemon syrup cake with raspberries. She adored raspberries. She perked up the instant the waiter reappeared, welcoming him with a beaming smile. With his eyes on her he asked if they wanted dessert or coffee.

Forgetting about the others, she ordered immediately. 'Can I have the lemon syrup cake with raspberries and boozy cream please? And—' with a conspiratorial smile she looked up at him '—can I have a little extra cream?'

The waiter smiled back. 'Of course.'

Lissa looked around the others expectantly and was disconcerted to find them all staring at her with slightly shocked expressions. She felt like a bug under a microscope.

'What?' she asked in confusion. 'Is that OK? I'm sorry. Don't we have time for dessert? Do we have to get back to the office?'

'No, it's fine,' Rory answered. He picked up the menu and glanced at it swiftly. 'I'll have the white chocolate and raspberry torte.'

'Just an espresso for me,' Marnie chimed in.

'Ditto,' added James.

'You're not having dessert?' Lissa asked Marnie incredulously after the waiter had left. 'I *never* miss dessert,' she declared emphatically.

Marnie laughed. 'Well, now we know how to keep you

happy. You've been quiet as a mouse all lunch and now dessert's on its way you've sprung to life.' She gave her a critical look. 'How do you stay so slim if you always eat dessert?'

Lissa shook her head with a smile. 'I'm not slim. I'm tall— more room to hide it.'

'No, you're slim,' Marnie disagreed. 'Do you work out?'

'No, I'm not a gym fan. I just walk the streets looking at things.'

She stole a quick glance at Rory and saw him smiling at her. 'Playing the tourist?'

'Absolutely,' she replied, tilting her chin.

James looked from Rory to her and back again. 'What do you do to keep fit, then, Rory? You're in good shape and still knock back dessert.'

'Rugby,' came the reply as Rory sat back for the waiter to present the dish.

'Rugby? You'll appreciate that, Lissa, coming from the land of the All Blacks,' James said, smiling at her with a touch of malice. 'Don't all Kiwi girls play rugby now too?'

'Actually, I think of it as Thugby,' Lissa said, concentrating on slicing her cake with a fork. 'All that macho male aggression, jumping on each other, mucking around in mud.' She rolled her eyes.

'Aren't you comfortable with macho men?' Rory challenged. 'Rugby is a good sport for us Neanderthal types. It provides a safe environment for us work off our energy and frustration.'

Her skin prickled. Frustration, huh? She couldn't stop raising her brows slightly. She glanced up at him and caught his fiery gaze on her.

'I can think of better ways to do that,' James said with his all too familiar lecherous tone.

Lissa ignored him, fascinated instead by the expression on

Rory's face. Amused, heated, knowing. They could all think of a better way to ease frustration, but, while it was James who would express it, it was Rory and Lissa who wanted to do it. She knew it and he knew it. But she couldn't let that happen.

Marnie filled the sudden silence. 'Are you looking forward to going home, Lissa?'

Rory looked back to his plate.

'Yes, I haven't been back since I left. It'll be nice to catch up with friends. There are still a million places I want to go to, but I can travel again some time.'

'You don't want to stay in London?'

She shrugged. 'Even if I wanted to I couldn't. My working visa expires in two months and then I'll have to leave.'

'You could always find yourself a British husband, Lissa. Then you could work anywhere in Europe for as long as you like.' James waggled his eyebrows. 'If you need someone for the job, just let me know.'

The expression of distaste Rory flicked at James was comical. Lissa gave them both a saccharine smile. 'Why, thank you anyway, James, but as I only intend to do it the once, if and when I marry it will be for love.'

She looked back at her plate, deciding to get what pleasure she could out of the wonderfully syrupy cake. The citrus scent reminded her of being in Rory's embrace and she indulged in the headiness of it. She ate each mouthful with relish until she was left with just a few berries and a pile of cream. Throwing all good manners aside, she put her fork down and picked up a single raspberry, swirling it in the cream, covering it completely. Happily she put it in her mouth and licked the remaining cream off her fingers. It was delicious. Just the right amount of liqueur had been added to the cream to give a sweet, warm tingle in the mouth. The tartness of the raspberry a perfect foil. Ignoring the others completely, she repeated the

procedure until the last of the berries was gone. Then she
dabbed her finger in the cream and licked it off, glancing up
and meeting Rory's eyes as she did so. The burning intensity
of his gaze shocked her and she lowered her hand nervously.
Desperately she tuned back into the conversation. Marnie and
James seemed to be talking tennis.

Lissa couldn't help but look over to where Rory was
dawdling his way through his dessert. 'What's the torte like?'

'Magnificent.' He looked at her with a sly smile. 'Want
to try some?'

'Oh, no,' she said immediately, shaking her head vehe-
mently. 'No. No, thanks.'

He picked up his fork and speared a piece with it. Then he
held it across the table towards her. 'Go on. You know you
want to.' His voice was as soft and tempting as the cake. His
eyes held the dare.

Staring across at him, she felt the dampened flick of desire
flame again. Damn, she shouldn't have been so greedy. With
his arm stretched across the table, in front of Marnie and
James, it was impossible for her to refuse. Carefully avoiding
contact with his fingers, she took the fork he held and lifted
it to her mouth. He was right, it was magnificent, but it did
nothing to assuage the hunger that clawed at her lower belly.

He was watching her intently. She handed the fork back,
uncomfortably aware of the intimacy of sharing it.

'Care for some more?' His voice was low and she couldn't
look away from him as she silently shook her head. She
sucked her lips in and pressed down on them, desperate not
to lick them and show the sexual tension she was feeling. But
she knew the action showed it anyway; his eyes flickered as
answering heat rose.

Marnie and James had fallen silent, and Lissa remembered
their presence with a start. 'Uh, you guys want to try some?'

she asked with pseudo-brightness trying to shake off the intense atmosphere that had descended over the table. Both declined. Lissa looked away, embarrassed.

James left to make a call while Marnie rose at the same time for a trip to the bathroom. Good manners required Lissa remain and keep Rory company as he slowly ate the rest of his torte.

He looked at her, his eyes focussed on her mouth. 'You have a little cream.' He raised his hand to his chin.

'Oh.' She lifted a hand and wiped at her own.

He smiled. 'No, you missed it. Here.' He reached across the table and ran his finger just under her lower lip.

She breathed in sharply and his finger stopped, still pressed against her. She wanted to taste him with her tongue. She parted her mouth to do just that, desperate to lick her lips, to be ready for him. There was a silence. Then he moved his finger again, upwards this time to stroke over her lip and back again. She sat frozen to the spot, melting.

'Tell me you don't want me to touch you,' he dared her softly.

Lissa had several talents, but lying wasn't one of them. Her eyes flickered and she was silent. He traced her lips again, the lightness of his touch a teasing torment. She wanted more. She wanted his lips on hers. She leaned closer, her eyes trained on his mouth.

'Lissa?' he breathed. 'Do you feel this? Do you?'

The rawness in his voice jerked at her.

'It's just sex.' She pulled back, desperate to retrieve the situation. She thought about blaming the boozy cream, but knew that had more aroma than impact.

He looked across at her, heat and amusement mingling in his gaze. 'If it's just sex, why don't we do something about it?'

She recoiled. Just have a fling? A one-night stand? Go for it like rabbits and get it out of their systems? Again, she was tempted. Damn tempted. She was leaving the country soon—

why not have an affair? Gina had suggested she do just that with Karl. Her heart thundered—too dangerous.

She looked at the table. He reached across to her again and tilted her chin up. She met his eyes, now glowing with heat and something else that she couldn't define—warmth? Gentleness? 'Because it's not just sex?' he said softly.

Her heart drowned in the knowledge that he was right. This attraction seemed to be more than just physical. Even more reason to say no. 'It can't happen, Rory.'

His hand dropped. 'Not until you say.'

When they returned to the office and resumed work things had changed. There was a lightening of the atmosphere between them. She had admitted to the attraction that he had so openly referred to earlier. And despite her intention to do nothing about it, it was a secret they shared, a bond between them. Their eyes met with silent laughter when James made one of his outrageous comments. Fingers brushed when they passed paperwork. She knew he watched her as surreptitiously and as often as she watched him. It was a dangerous game but she thought that she could just, just keep a lid on it. Keep things as they were. They had acknowledged the temptation, but that was as far as it would go. For sure.

Before home time she asked him to check some figures she'd inputted into one of the databases. Standing behind her, he leant over her shoulder, pointing at the screen. She had to forcibly stop herself leaning even closer. She could feel the heat of his body behind her. It would take nothing to lean back against him, to feel him hard against her just as she'd been dreaming, night after night.

He seemed to sense she'd lost her concentration on the work. 'What shampoo do you use? Your hair smells delicious.'

'It's called Esprit de Fleur. You can buy it in the supermarket for five ninety-nine.' She couldn't stop the tart reply, a gut defence against his nearness, a way of trying to push him away because if she didn't she was in grave danger of pulling him closer—literally, physically, now.

She felt his withdrawal and knew he was about to walk away and suddenly that prospect was worse.

'I don't suggest you do, though.' She quickly turned to him.

'Why not?' He came tantalisingly close again, his attention trained on her.

She looked back at her screen. 'Whatever you currently use suits you.'

'It does?'

'Mmm,' she answered as matter of factly as she could, despite her thumping heart and the audible catch in her voice. 'Lemony. It's nice. Fresh.'

'You noticed?'

I notice everything about you. To say that would be to go too far. She was playing with fire already and she knew it. Trouble was, it was irresistible. He was irresistible.

He lingered, perhaps waiting for another move, another sign from her. So with superhuman strength she kept her focus on the computer, wishing the others hadn't left already, until finally, after what seemed like eons of sweet torture, he lifted away and went to sit back at his own screen.

She breathed out. Close, too close and yet not nearly close enough. Mentally she begged for the fortnight to pass fast; every day was killing her. Why was it you always wanted what you couldn't have?

Rory decided to take the stairs back up to the office after the breakfast meeting with the client. Anything to burn off the excess energy and frustration welling in him. Damn it. The situation was eating him up and he was struggling to concentrate on the project. So much for forgetting about her until it had wrapped. Who the hell was he kidding?

He wasn't the most arrogant guy, but he knew when someone was interested, and she wanted him. He'd seen the way she watched him, the way she flushed when he stood near her, had felt her tremble as his hand brushed hers when working at her computer together.

She'd even admitted it—tried to fob it off as just sexual attraction. But it was more than that. He'd yet to figure out quite how much more, but definitely more. Not just attraction but undeniable need, he had to get closer to her. His body screamed for it. The frustration that she wouldn't give in to it was almost greater than the frustration that he felt from not being with her. It was like being tortured on the rack, slow and painful.

Hell, he should never have commandeered her for his team, but he hadn't been able to stop himself, the temptation to have her near too great. But he hadn't banked on how totally it affected his concentration. Then again, if she weren't under his nose he'd be spending his days wondering about her.

He'd never been bewitched before. It was humiliating and he needed to do something about it. He knew exactly what he *wanted* to do, but he had to understand her resistance to conquer it.

It wasn't as if she was totally off men. Hell, she even had Gina trying to matchmake her with her mate. He ran up the first flight of stairs swiftly, deep in thought.

All this rubbish about office gossip was a smokescreen. She was a temp, for goodness' sake; she'd be heading home to New Zealand in no time. Why care what a bunch of people here thought when soon she'd be out of the place?

They could have a lot of fun together before she did take off. She should be taking in all the experiences London had to offer. He was determined to be one of those experiences.

So if not fear of gossip, then fear of what? He could do scared; hell he was a little scared himself. He'd never felt a pull like this. He could give her time if that was what she needed. Some time anyway. OK, maybe not much more time.

He mulled over that first night they'd met. She'd been so funny. So damn sexy. Her hair loose, her tongue loose. He smirked—very loose. He couldn't believe she was the same woman so buttoned up in the office the next day. Hair swept back, a frosty manner. That wasn't really her. No, the hints of the tantalising, enthusiastic siren underneath were all too clear. Her cynical amusement at the competitive interplay between James and Marnie, the enthusiastic way she ate her dessert, her passion for the city, the lust in her eyes when they touched. She wore stockings and suspenders, for heaven's sake. The woman was a sensualist hiding behind ice.

Bounding up the fourth flight of stairs, he decided he must remember to keep raspberries and cream in the fridge. Watching her eat that dessert with her fingers had given him the biggest hard-on he'd had in years. He'd had to take ages over his own cake to give himself time to regain control before they stood up at the table. Control. Was that what she was afraid of losing? What he could do to her to make her lose control. He ached to do it, every wild fantasy spinning in his head.

She needed a shake-up. He wanted to strip away that frost, strip away that fear and then strip her, literally. He laughed at his crassness.

Running up the next flight, he looked up and his heart seized in his chest. Suddenly he was as breathless as if he'd been running a marathon. There she was, standing at the landing at the top, staring at him, her hand clenched on the banister. He stopped and eyeballed her. Perfect. Time for a little conversation. Without breaking eye contact he slowly climbed the remaining five steps to stand on the step just below her. It almost brought them to eye level. Her mouth only an inch or two below his. Perfect positioning.

He breathed deeply a couple of times and studied her. She was breathing as hard as him and she'd only come down six stairs. It pleased him. He got to her, just as she did him. She sucked her beautiful pouty lips into her mouth again, pressing on them as if she was holding back the words. He wanted to free them with his finger, to feel the soft fullness. He wanted her to say whatever it was on her mind.

He decided to cut right to the chase. Her hand still gripped the banister. He covered it with one of his own. It trembled.

'I think it's time we faced up to this, don't you?'

Her eyes darkened.

So did his mood. 'Tell me why not.'

'You're my boss.'

Bingo. An honest reason and one he felt compelled to overcome. 'That's just a situation.'

'It's unethical.'

'No, it's not. It happens all the time.'

'That doesn't make it right. There's an imbalance of…power.'

'I wouldn't abuse that and, even if I tried, you wouldn't let me.'

A shadow crossed her face. His heart pounded. They could get over this. They had to.

The direction of her gaze transfixed him. Slowly it lifted from his mouth to his eyes and he could see the golden flickers of light burning in the depths of the warm brown.

He was desperate to touch her. Desperate to wrap his arms around her, kiss her. He forced himself to go slowly. Move gently. He couldn't afford to scare her off him any more than she was already. He cursed the circumstances in which they'd met. It wasn't great for him either.

'OK,' he said softly. He climbed the final step, taking her

hand off the banister with his and walking towards her. She stepped backwards. He kept walking. Forcing her across the little landing until her back was against the wall. He took another step nearer so only a fraction of air hung between them. He kept hold of her hand, his thumb stroking her wrist. He could feel her pulse hammering. He stared down at her, searching her eyes. The spark of defiance was there, but so was the heat and suddenly it was all heat. Satisfaction settled into him.

'We're both adults. We're on equal footing,' he said in a low voice.

She opened her mouth to argue and he stopped her the best way he knew. She melted into him immediately, her yielding sigh spilling in his embrace. His already hard body tightened further in response. Her mouth was so soft, so sweet as it opened for him. He fought for the strength to be gentle, not to ravish as his inner caveman wanted him to. But he couldn't stop the escalation. Couldn't control his desire to touch her everywhere, especially *there*. He'd been dreaming about it for nights, remembering the sensation as his fingers had skimmed from soft silk to even softer skin.

He reached down, sliding his hands under her skirt and slowly up her thighs. He had to know. Yes, there it was. His fingers reached the top of her stockings and flowed onto bare skin. The jolt of desire toppled his self-control and he groaned against her. She rotated her hips against him and he knew she wanted more. The floodgates had been opened and she was kissing him as hard and as hungrily as he kissed her. Her fingers pulled in his hair, holding him to her. He loved it. He ground his hips into hers and his senses sky-rocketed when she rocked viciously back against him.

His fingers traced up alongside the suspender strap. She parted her legs to give him greater access. He slid sideways until he reached the lacy edge of her panties.

He was certain she felt it as badly as he did. Wanted it as badly. He wanted to talk to her, to say it, to hear her say it, but he couldn't bear to tear his lips from her silky skin and that reddened mouth. He teased her, running his fingers along the elastic of her underwear, and felt her try to spread her legs further against the tightness of her skirt.

He let her pull back from his kiss to gasp for air, pressing his mouth along the length of her throat as her head fell back to rest against the wall. Still his fingers teased even though her gasps and wriggling hips told him of her growing impatience. He smiled against the skin exposed at the top of her shirt, breathing in her flowery freshness. And then he felt her hands on the back of his thighs, felt the heat from them through his trousers as they swooped upwards, felt the pressure as they squeezed his butt, and he knew he was in trouble. Inner caveman began to assert dominance. Enough teasing. He cupped her mound with the flat of his palm, while stroking his fingers lower, deeper between her legs; he felt the dampness through the silk and lace and almost shook with need. He very nearly ripped the fabric away so he could taste her there with his mouth.

Then he heard it. The slamming of the stairwell door above. He pulled away from her, staring into her eyes. She stared back at him in confusion, the dazed look almost killing him. He wanted to keep going so bad. But not now, not here. He jerked his head in the direction that footsteps were approaching. He saw her eyes widen in shock as she registered their downward descent.

'Damn,' he muttered, wanting to swear far harder and louder. She pulled at her skirt in panic and deftly he took her by the arm and led her down. They seemed to fly. Excitement drove him. She couldn't deny it now. She was as hot for him as he was for her. Lovers. He could hardly wait.

He swiped his pass and opened the door to the basement, pulling her inside, desperate to get that close to her again. Not wanting the brief moments apart to have given her a chance to build walls again.

Too late. She'd already skated out of his grasp and was facing him square with the icy barriers back in place.

'I thought you said you weren't going to touch me again unless I asked you to.' She'd whispered, but it echoed anyway in the dimly lit concrete car park. *Touch me, touch me.* It was all he heard, all he wanted to hear.

'You asked.' It came out low and rough. He knew he was in dangerous waters with this whole boss/temp thing. Knew her discomfort about it was partly justified. Damn, but he'd been told she was right for the project and he'd wanted the chance to get to know her. And for that he needed time. Contact time. The sooner the job wrapped, the better; he'd make sure they weren't assigned to the same one again.

She glared at him, her eyebrows raised, but the fire in her eyes wasn't all anger.

'You asked.' He repeated with more confidence than he felt. He wished he could just pull her into his arms again and show her, but the moment had passed.

She made to refute but he held his hands up to silence her. Then he pointed to her face. 'You asked with your eyes.'

Her gaze dropped instantly, her pale eyelids hiding the gold-flecked brown orbs that told him so much. He saw her struggling, saw how much this thing between them affected her. Well, she wasn't the only one thrown for a loop. He shoved the inner caveman back behind his rock and aimed to lighten the moment.

'Don't worry,' he said with a laugh that sounded as forced as it was. 'Next time I'll wait to hear the request.'

She looked up then and he almost gasped at the torture in

her expression. She looked so torn. He wished she'd talk to him. Wanted her to open her heart and mind to him as much as he wanted her to open her body. He wanted the whole damn lot from her. Everything.

Hell, that was a first.

For a moment it looked as if she was going to say something, but then she bit on her lips, the action almost driving him to break his word. He said nothing as she walked past him and re-entered the stairwell. He stood, trying to catch breath, trying to the control the Eiffel Tower in his pants enough to be able to walk up the damn stairs again, let alone return to his desk and concentrate to some degree on work.

God help him if she never did ask.

CHAPTER FOUR

OUT of the corner of her eye Lissa watched Rory. He looked deep in thought, frowning at his laptop. She had avoided him as far as possible since the incident in the stairwell. She'd spent the weekend sightseeing in Bath with a girl-friend and had almost succeeded in forgetting about Rory for a three-hour period. The rest of the time he'd been foremost in her thoughts.

Back at the office on Monday the work had cranked up. Now the presentation to the client was only two days away and they were working round the clock. She'd been able to slip home ahead of him. Marnie and James were constant fixtures at their desks so they were never alone. Besides, she had the distinct impression he was waiting for her to make the next move. Fine. All she had to do was ensure she didn't make it even if that was the toughest thing she'd ever had to do. Far tougher than walking out on her life nearly two years ago.

She'd told him the reason she couldn't be with him. But she hadn't realised the extent of her own vulnerability to him. Within two seconds of his touch she'd been his. Uncaring about how little she knew about him, uncaring of the fact that they had been in a public area and could have been caught at any moment. Almost had been, in fact. If he hadn't acted they would have been. He'd been far more grounded than her and that terrified her.

He'd said she'd asked him to touch her and she knew he was right. In her mind she'd been begging and he'd read it. What a mistake. They'd discovered her weakness together. That he just had to touch her and all her resistance melted. She was not going to risk ruining her career a second time. She wanted to end this contract on a high, not a messy low. But even more scary was the depth of her reaction to him. It didn't seem normal. This wasn't your average case of the hots. She knew that if she gave into it she would be on the road for major heartache. A distraction for him seemed to be something more for her and she was too afraid to analyse exactly what.

So she reverted to ice-princess mode again, unable to meet his eyes for fear of what she might see there or, worse, what she might give away. Marnie and James were too busy to notice. And, perhaps, so was Rory.

Suppressing a sigh, she went to find Gina for five minutes' light relief. She stole a look as she passed him on the way out and caught him staring at her with an expression of such want that she felt herself blush all over. Her eyes darted back to the door ahead. Not too busy.

Gina, happy to hang for a moment, gave her a concerned look. 'Hey, come on, they're having drinks down the pub tonight. One of the other projects has wrapped. Come and have a few and relax.'

Lissa opened her mouth to refuse and suddenly thought better of it. 'Good idea.' These last few days she'd been working so hard she had been feeling almost reclusive. She was supposed to be making the most of her last few weeks—she should be out and about every night instead of lying awake for hours at a stretch dreaming about a guy she shouldn't and couldn't have.

A night out with Gina and the gang would be a great way

of relaxing. Rory and the others should be working late again, so no fear of having to see even more of him.

'Good, you're looking too pale and miserable. You need a good night out.'

Lissa attempted a grin back, forcing levity into her voice. 'You know, you're absolutely right.'

A few drinks, get the whole Rory thing into perspective.

Rory knew the minute the door opened that she was back. He could tell her soft step on the carpet, could smell the freshness that was uniquely her. Clenching his jaw, he welded himself to the spot, refusing to turn around and take in the view as he really wanted.

He looked across at James, who was openly appraising Lissa. Irritation flared again. He didn't like the way James looked at Lissa, uncomfortably aware that it was exactly how he looked at her himself—with lust. But James, he knew, was only about lust, whereas increasingly he wanted to understand the whole package. Something about her got to him, and made him want her more than he'd wanted any woman.

Next thing he knew she was approaching him waving a piece of paper.

'Rory, I need you to sign my timesheet for last week. I need to fax it in to the agency this afternoon to be sure I get paid. I forgot to get you to do it on Friday and I've only just remembered.'

Well, he knew exactly why that was. Friday. The stairs. He looked up into her face. She was staring at the paper she'd laid on the desk next to him. Not giving anything away. She hadn't since those stolen moments in the stairwell, moments that he'd been replaying twenty-four seven ever since. He cursed the interruption, desperately dreaming up ways in which he could try it again. The desire to touch her so overwhelmed him, it threatened his work and he hated that. A large part of him hated the effect she had on him.

No way was he seriously drawn to her, was he? Not someone who, frankly, could be more than a little stroppy. Well, yes. Besides, he had a feeling the stroppiness was related to the battle to keep him at a distance. Once they were over that, he was more than aware of the ways she would be able to make up for it. She was fun. He saw the amusement, the humour, all too often in her expression. Why couldn't they have a couple of months' excitement?

Realising he'd been staring at her for far too long and that as a result her face now glowed rosily, he jerked his attention from her to the page before him. He gave it a perfunctory scan before adding his signature to the bottom line. Then something caught his eye.

'Your full name is Lisette?' He didn't exactly know hundreds, but he'd never come across a New Zealander with a French-sounding name before.

'My father was French Canadian.'

He digested that for a moment. 'Was?'

She nodded and he saw the brightness in her face dim.

'Did you learn French?'

'No. Actually he died before I was born.' The shadows in her eyes grew darker. The golden flecks faded in brilliance.

'That must have been hard on your mother.'

'It was. But she was a survivor.'

'Was?' His heart thumped a little harder. He didn't mean to pry, but he knew he was getting information that was vital. Clues that might help him understand the faint sense of mystery about her. Some fact that might help him figure out why she was so reluctant to follow what he knew she wanted. What his heart and body wanted so much.

'Was.' She snatched the paper up and walked away from

him. He quietly watched her as she sat back down in her chair, avoiding looking anywhere in particular, especially at him.

An orphan. Fatherless from birth and motherless since— when? The questions nearly burst forth, but her shuttered expression told him he'd got as far as he was going to—for today anyway.

He went back to the figures on the screen in front of him and for the first time in his career wished his work away. Wanted the project to be over so he could have the time to focus on her. Disgusted, he jabbed at the keyboard. What on earth had come over him? He'd said quite clearly he didn't want distractions. But meeting Lissa was more than a distraction. It felt like a life-changing event, one beyond his control and one he wasn't sure he could handle.

Lissa escaped earlier than she'd thought she'd be able to, leaving the others up to their elbows in charts. She raced along the footpath to Jackson's, the bar where Gina and the others were already on their second round. Gina waved her over excitedly and Lissa was soon ensconced with fresh pineapple juice in hand, slightly distanced persona in place talking with some of the junior consultants.

Suddenly she felt an elbow in her ribs. 'Come and meet Karl.' Gina had such an expectant look on her face as she dragged Lissa near the door that Lissa had to stifle a giggle. She recognised him from the party at the office where she had mistaken him for Rory. She cringed afresh at her blunder. While Karl had a great physique and a fabulously cheeky grin, he was no Rory. They were poles apart in terms of dynamism and sheer animal magnetism.

Karl took her hand and gave her the benefit of the cheeky charmer grin. 'Great to meet you at last. I've heard so much about you.'

'As I have you.' Lissa smiled at him. She was surprised as she caught the vestige of a wink. Not a suggestive wink, but more one aimed at a co-conspirator. That was funny. Unless she was reading things wrong this guy wasn't interested in meeting someone new in the least. She sipped from her glass, appreciating her decision to go with the refreshing juice, watching the interplay between him and Gina.

Gina was her usual bubbly self, but Lissa noticed the serious glint in Karl's eye as he watched her. It took about fifteen seconds of observing this for her to make the connection. Gina disappeared, called away by another friend, and Lissa lost no time in calling him to account.

'You've fallen for Gina, haven't you?' She looked at him full on.

He stared back, his eyes widening a fraction before looking away to where Gina stood chatting safely out of earshot. 'Guilty as charged.'

She saw the flicker of insecurity flash before he hid it behind a self-deprecating smile.

'Waste of time, though, when she's only interested in types like him.'

She glanced around to where he was looking and drew a painful breath. Rory had arrived and was standing next to Gina and staring at them with a thunderous expression. She felt floored by the ferocity of his gaze. She turned back quickly, looking down at her drink, feeling the heat in her cheeks. What was he doing here? She'd thought she was in the clear for just a few hours. Her Rory-Proximity Indicator, aka her pulse, started its crazy zigzag. She found her attraction to him so hard to control and she knew it would only take a moment alone with him for it to snap. She had to prevent that from happening.

'Hmm.' Karl grunted.

Lissa could just about hear the cogs creaking as they turned in his brain.

'Who is he?' he asked.

'Rory. One of the bosses.' She said it to remind herself more than to inform him. 'Look, great to meet you, Karl, but I need to head home.'

With a wave she left him and started to move towards Gina to say goodnight.

Rory stepped in front of her, blocking her slow trail across the room, his chest a more effective barrier than the Great Wall of China. 'So Gina was right, then?' He asked, his voice rasping harshly.

'About what?' she asked cautiously. She'd never seen him look so grim.

'That he'd be the perfect good-time guy for you.' He jerked his head in Karl's direction. Anger oozed from every pore.

If she weren't so strung out she'd have laughed. Instead she sighed. Their situation was fractious enough without having unwarranted jealousy compounding it.

'Actually, no, she wasn't right about that.'

The hardness in his eyes remained.

'But she was right about one thing,' she continued, the need to set him at ease overruling her plan to keep him at a distance.

'What's that?'

'You do have the most amazing eyes.' She looked at him and let her attraction shine out clearly. Time stopped and, fascinated, she watched as his expression softened from anger to amusement and then to desire. The unspoken communication held them in thrall. She felt heat mount in her cheeks and a thrilling tingle rippled through her as she saw an answering flush rise in his. The desire she had been trying so desperately to hold in check this last week was spiralling upwards—again.

She finally recognised that it was never going to go away

of its own accord. The feelings she thought she could control were not lessening with each day. Instead the attraction mounted. With every day came new knowledge, more familiarity, more fun. And the need to be one with him grew. It felt inevitable. Uncontrollable.

She didn't want him thinking she was even remotely interested in Karl. The idea was laughable. Right now she felt as if she'd never want anyone the way she wanted Rory. The thought scared her half to death.

Finally she spoke, a whisper. 'I'm going home.'

'Let me come with you.' An equally quiet whisper.

A wry smile lifted the corners of her mouth. 'No one's coming tonight.'

A rueful look crossed his face. She knew he'd caught her *double entendre*. 'More's the pity.' Regret swirled between them.

'What's happened? Don't tell me the computers have crashed and we've lost the reports?' James broke in on them, his hilarity jarring her back to her surroundings. He stood with a drink in each hand, brows raised, flicking his glance from one to the other in query. She glanced back at Rory. He'd retreated and was looking coldly at James who was still talking. 'You need a drink, Lissa?'

She shook her head. 'I'm just leaving. See you tomorrow.' She walked away before either of them could say anything more.

She waved goodbye to Gina, who came to meet her at the door.

'People are asking if you and Rory are having an affair,' Gina said without preamble.

Lissa's head jerked back.

'Don't get mad,' Gina added hurriedly. 'I've said not as far as I knew. I just thought you'd like to know.'

Lissa forced herself to shrug. It was hardly surprising. Even Karl had immediately spotted the attraction between them. Coupled with the few incidents in front of Marnie and James and the soul-searching looks they'd just swapped in the middle of the crowded bar, of course people were going to wonder. Despite what she'd said to Rory, she didn't really care. People would think what they liked with little regard for the truth. She'd learnt that one a long time ago as the only child of a single teenage mother. Besides, it wouldn't be the only office affair to be speculated on and nor would it be the last. There'd be another shortly, she bet, knowing the antics of some of the junior consultants.

'Are you OK?' Gina touched her arm, bringing her back to the here and now. 'Look, Lissa, if you don't want to tell me, fine. But I know there's something going on. You guys put all the "izzle" in sizzle.'

Lissa smiled, aiming for nonchalance, unwilling to unload the sorry saga onto Gina. 'I'm fine. Just tired, that's all. I'm going to call it a night.'

Thursday passed in a flash. Despite another night of minimal sleep, she sped through the final version of the reports. By mid afternoon they'd been checked and she was printing and binding copies to be distributed at the presentation.

Then she set about perfecting the online slide show and ensuring that the equipment Rory and the others needed to take with them on Friday had been checked by IT and was ready to go. The others had been in conference at the other end of the table for most of the afternoon. Lissa glanced down at them, taking a breather from the figures in front of her. They all seemed hyped on an adrenaline rush. Rory's energy levels were phenomenal. He paced the end of the room, eyes gleaming as he grilled Marnie over and over on her part of the presentation. He seemed to thrive on the excitement of the challenge. Looked so competent, so assured, so focussed.

Lissa grimaced and looked back at her computer. She felt anything but—her suit crumpled rather than crisp, her body hot and sticky. Her throat was sore and her head felt heavy and seemed to have the army band drumming in it. Even her eyeballs ached. She put her hands to her cheeks; they were burning up and her cold fingers soothed them a little.

She was tired. Tired of staring at computer screen and graphs and figures for hours, tired of being cooped up in this tiny room, but most of all she was tired of being so close to Rory and yet not being with him. She wanted him. Badly. The thought consumed her and so did the resulting anger. She was allowing her physical attraction to him to overshadow her work. Such a thing had never happened before. The thought of him fevered her mind. It clouded her judgment and, she worried, affected her performance. She resented his ability to be able to switch it off. How could he be so focussed on work if he felt the same overwhelming passion?

Suddenly it was well after six and the office had all but emptied leaving just their small team. Marnie and James went to get pizza, insisting on going out to get it rather than order delivery. Marnie said she was desperate for fresh air. James took the orders. Distractedly Lissa said she'd be happy with anything but seafood. Damn, she needed to get this finished so she could get away. Her nerves were shot to pieces. It was all she could do to sit there and keep some semblance of concentration on the screen.

She battled to finish the remaining few pages. Part of her wanted to get out of the room and head for home as fast as possible and the other part wanted nothing more than to leap onto Rory and ravish him. Her reservations about an office fling were fading fast under the weight of the desire she felt for him. They would only have a few weeks together. But then that was a whole problem in itself. As the days progressed and her attraction steadily grew she knew she had to be stronger than ever because she could end up heartbroken. Total no-win situation.

She wanted him so badly but she couldn't have him.

A heavy silence filled the room. She sat fuming at the apparent ease with which he could continue working. He had such focus despite her proximity whereas she was practically having a meltdown. She couldn't resist jibing at him.

'People are saying we're having an affair.' Her tone was as bitter as burnt coffee grinds.

'Really?' Rory didn't look up from his screen. 'I'm surprised. They know I don't usually fool around in the office.'

'And why don't you *usually*?' Lissa demanded, anger sparking within her.

'Work's work and play's play,' he replied easily, his eyes still fixed on the computer before him.

'And never the twain shall meet?' she asked tartly. She wasn't sure why, but she felt the need to goad him. To prove he wasn't as immune as he appeared.

'It's easier that way. Otherwise how do you concentrate on work?' Suddenly he jerked his head up and glared at her. She shrank at the blaze in his eyes. He continued, his volume rising with every word. 'How do you cope if the woman you've fallen for is sitting across from you, only inches away, and yet you can't reach out and touch her the way you want to? How the *hell* do you get any work done?' He swore viciously and pushed the keyboard away.

Satisfaction slammed into her. But still she continued prodding brazenly. 'So you'd rather out of sight, out of mind?'

'No,' he replied with a mirthless laugh. 'Never out of mind. But it makes it damn hard to concentrate on bloody numbers when you're wearing a slightly see-through blouse and all I want to do is rip it off to see what's underneath it properly.'

Heat consumed her. Heart thudding, she stood and reached for her suit jacket. Just as quickly he rose and came around the table. He reached out a hand and grasped her wrist. His grip was hard. Her jacket fell to the floor. They stood staring at each other. She was certain he could feel the frantic tempo of her pulse. She watched as he lowered his gaze to her lips, then down to her chest. With a deep breath she realised her breasts had tightened and swollen. He stared at them and they tightened still further. With her arm outstretched pulling the fabric of her shirt taut across her body, she knew there was no way he could fail to see their aroused outline. He looked back up at her face. His pupils were so large there was only the smallest ring of dazzling emerald around them.

'Feeling cold?' he mocked.

Desire and anger merged and grew. She was so close to the edge. She sucked her lips in and bit down on them, trying to suppress the throbbing desire, wishing the pressure on them could be his lips rather than her own teeth. Then she took a breath. 'Practically hypothermic.'

The hint of a smile softened his blazing stare. The pressure of his hand on her wrist grew and he pulled her towards him. His other hand came up and cradled her jaw, his thumb sweeping down from her cheek to her chin in soft strokes.

'Why do you care so much what they think? You don't do what you *want* because you think people might say something behind your back. Why should you even care?'

She stared up at him. He was wrong. It wasn't about other people. She didn't do what she wanted because she knew from past experience that it would be the worst thing for her. An office affair was a fantasy that invariably ended as a nightmare. The environment was false; you worked as a close unit for a short time, living in each other's pockets. Adrenaline and excitement gave an unnatural high. It wasn't the real world and who knew what secrets were in Rory's life outside the office? What would happen when he was locked away in another project room with another temp he might find attractive?

His thumb continued its gentle stroking. The response in her bones was not so gentle. Despite what her brain was telling her, she wanted him badly.

'Let's really give them something to talk about,' he said softly, his focus on her mouth. His thumb stroked her lips. They parted a fraction. He stroked his thumb across again, pushing it in slightly so she felt it brush against her tongue. Her desire to taste him intimately flared.

'If they're all thinking it, it seems a shame not to make the most of it.' He looked down at her, hesitating.

'What do you want from me?' She stared at him, feeling tortured.

He looked at her with such solemn intensity that she knew she was about to get a painfully honest answer.

'Everything. I want to touch you, taste you. I want to see you writhe in pleasure. I want to see you lose control.'

'Why?' She barely recognised the croaky whisper as her own.

He gave a wry smile. 'It would make me feel good.'

'What—to have control over me?'

'No.' His eyes darkened in frustration. 'Not like that. I want to know that I can touch you in ways that drive you crazy, that I can satisfy you.'

Her eyes widened in surprise. She didn't try to hide it. Her head ached and she was using all her energy to stay on her feet. She couldn't possibly hide anything from him right now. She answered huskily. 'You should know that already.'

His eyes blazed, boring into hers. 'Are you going to let me?'

'I don't think I have much choice.'

He growled. 'Of course you do. You decide.'

'I'm sick of fighting it.'

'Fighting me?'

'No, fighting me.'

His thumb continued rubbing her jaw gently and his gaze dropped to her mouth again.

She knew he wanted to kiss her but he held firm, watching, waiting for her to acquiesce. He seemed to be holding heaven out to her and all she had to do was lean forward and take it from him. The long days and even longer nights of loneliness and want and need overwhelmed her. She blanked the future, no longer caring, no longer able to think. All that mattered right now was this.

Her control snapped. 'I want you to touch me,' she whispered fiercely. 'I want you.'

She didn't just agree, she became the aggressor. It was what she had been wanting for so long. With a speed and strength that surprised both of them she reached up and ran both hands through his hair, pulling his head down to meet her hungry mouth. She licked and tasted him. Vaguely she heard him groan and then she moaned in delight as he pulled her hard up against him. They met length to length. She let him take her weight. He held her easily. The pressure of his hard chest against her sensitive breasts was dynamite. She squirmed her hips against his, her delight at feeling his arousal rendering her unable to control her writhing action. They were the perfect height for each other. Her long legs ensured that they met in the middle, just where they were supposed to. He put his hands on her hips and gripped hard, holding her while he slowly rocked against her, simulating the closer connection that she craved. And all the while their lips, teeth and tongues swirled and danced in a kiss so passionate she never wanted it to end, never wanted any of it to end.

But it wasn't enough. She was desperate to feel his bare skin against hers. Desperate to have him touch her intimately, taste her, suck her, fill her. She tugged at his shirt and moaned in frustration when it wouldn't give. He pulled back from her slightly.

'Lissa,' he said raggedly. 'Lissa, we can't.'

It was not what she wanted to hear. A feral growl escaped her and she reached up for him again. He held his head back firmly. 'They might come back any minute.'

Who? she wondered, half crazed. Right now she didn't give a damn.

He swore softly. 'Hell, beautiful, why did you have to pick tonight of all nights?' He stared into her eyes, and her need must have been clearly evident. 'I'll give you what you want, honey,' he whispered softly as he stood back from her a fraction. And then his warm, strong hand slid down the waistband of her skirt and straight into her panties. She gasped in surprise. His palm pressed hard against her and his fingers delved lower, stroking those lips. Her legs buckled and he caught her with his other arm. He backed her up so she was pressing against the table. Her legs spread wide of their own volition and she found herself leaning back on her hands before she knew it. He kept his hand where it was and his fingers started stroking rhythmically. He bent over her and claimed her mouth once more. His other hand lifted and caressed her breast, teasing the already hard nipple—swirling around it, rubbing, gently squeezing. Her whole body shook with delight, her aching mind relieved of thought, only capable of absorbing the sensations he incited.

After a few heavenly minutes she wrenched her mouth free of his, gasping for air. His lips trailed across her jaw and down her neck. Big, open-mouthed kisses that alternately sucked and soothed. She was on fire, in ecstasy and hurtling towards oblivion. Her breathless gasps accelerated to audible moans as his fingers continued their erotic torment and his thumb rotated around her sensitive nub. It made her want more, much more. She wanted everything. She stirred against him, and murmuring against her, he upped the pressure and pace.

The tempo and volume of her soft moans increased accordingly and she threw her head back, her hips bucking as her body tensed, on the edge of release. The cry of pleasure already building in her chest.

Then he was gone. Without warning he'd pulled back and with a muttered oath whipped his hand free.

'No!' she moaned, frantic. Just a few seconds more, just one second more!

'What is it with us and timing?' He grasped her shoulders and stood her upright, then quickly turned and pulled her chair out for her. She practically fell into it, breathless and stunned and so, so frustrated. She had been so close to what would have been the most powerful orgasm of her life. She sat dazed, wondering what the hell had just happened. Then she heard them. Voices, along the corridor. Rory must have heard the elevator bell.

'Come home with me tonight,' he said urgently in a low voice as he dug his hand into his pocket and pulled out a handkerchief before sliding into his own seat. He looked across at her, his eyes stormy and brilliant.

She stared at him, barely able to breathe let alone think or reply. Suddenly her headache came pounding back, blindingly vicious. The euphoria of the previous moment vanished and the void was rapidly filled with an icy cold. What was she doing? The emptiness was unbearable. She stared at him as horror sank in. Her uncontrollable desire for him appalled her. She was far on the road of no return and she needed to fight it. Fight hard. She curled her shaking hands into fists on her lap. She opened her mouth, bracing herself for her reply. She needed to shoot this down *now*.

The door opened and in walked James and Marnie bearing

large pizza boxes. The smell hit Lissa like a wall of slime. Disgusting.

She didn't stop working as they ate, knowing she was on borrowed time for getting the last of the work done before this headache rendered her utterly useless. She nodded as James set a piece of pizza beside her, but ignored it completely as she desperately focussed on ensuring there were no errors whatsoever in the final version.

Finally she sighed and clicked the save icon for what she hoped would be the last time. 'Can someone check this? I think I'm done here.'

Marnie came straight over waving another slice of pizza at her. Lissa shook her head and winced as pain knifed through her temple.

'Are you OK?' Marnie asked.

'Fine,' she replied softly, aware that Rory's head had jerked up at the question. She could sense his scrutiny.

Marnie watched over her shoulder as she scrolled through the pages. 'Looks great to me. Awesome. You are done!' she said at the conclusion.

Lissa let out a breath in relief and began to tidy away her things. Her hands shook slightly as she tried to work methodically through the pile.

Marnie's voice seemed to come from a distance. 'Hey, you're really flushed. Are you sure you're OK?'

She looked up and summoned the strength from who knew where to reply. 'It's just a headache.' She waved a vague hand at the computers. 'All that staring at the screen.'

Marnie smiled and nodded. 'Go home and SLEEP. You're so lucky this is all finished for you tonight. We've still got the big exam in the morning.'

She smiled weakly. Yes, for her it was over. Tomorrow she'd be back at her usual desk in the information centre. HQ would be a plain old meeting room again. The paper removed from the windows. Rory would be working on the floor below. The soreness in her throat sharpened.

'Is there anything else you'd like me to do?' her voice rasped. She avoided looking at Rory by fussing with her bag.

'No,' she heard him say quietly. 'You've done more than enough for tonight. We can take it from here.' He paused. 'Thank you.'

Did she imagine that tender stress in the way he said thank you? She couldn't bear it. As she reached the door she turned and addressed the room in general. 'Good luck for tomorrow.'

By the time she got home she was shaking head to toe. Alternately hot then cold, it was all she could do to get a glass of water, strip off her suit, pull an old tee shirt on and collapse into bed. Restful sleep eluded her. Flashes of moments with Rory span chaotically in her mind. She relived snatches of their meetings, the flare between them. She tossed and turned, her body either aching or on fire. It was close to dawn and the birds had started chirping when she finally descended into a dreamless sleep.

CHAPTER FIVE

RORY ran up the stairs back at the office with more energy than a nuclear reactor. The blood in his veins sang. He felt vitally alive and his excitement was palpable. James and Marnie had fed off it too. The meeting had been fantastic. The client had bought it hook, line and sinker and awarded a massive project to Franklin. He'd proved his right to win that promotion well and truly.

And now he was going to win what he'd really been racing for. Lissa. No holding back. Last night, she'd blown him away. So passionate. So damn hot. Utterly on fire for him. He'd nearly lost all reason and had her on the table then and there. How good that would have looked when James and Marnie walked back in with that pizza.

He laughed aloud exultantly. He'd hardly slept but he wouldn't have with the meeting today anyway. He didn't mind that it had scuppered the chance of being with her last night. It made the prospect of tonight even more exciting. It felt as if he'd wanted her for ever. It had been good to have the presentation to concentrate on in the end; reciting facts and figures had been a way to finally get to sleep rather than twisting and turning all night with the most enormous erection of his life. Of course, he'd been dreaming of her when he woke. The ache in his body had been growing since the night he first met her. She was so alive. So refreshingly blunt. Her laughter. So sexy with those long legs and caramel hair. But her reluctance in the office nearly killed him. It was all he could do to stop himself from teasing her, tormenting her into betraying herself. Making her reveal the sparkle and enthusiasm he knew bubbled under that cool façade.

His body tightened at the thought of the night to come. Unbuttoned and tousled. Oh, yes, it was all going to happen. After her response last night he knew she wouldn't say no to him.

He wasn't sure what she'd wanted to do just as the others got back. He'd seen the fear in her eyes and guessed she wanted to try to push him away again. But she couldn't. She'd opened up to him and going back now was impossible. He *knew*. He knew her passion for him was as blazing as his for her. And she knew he knew.

He strode into the library wanting to establish a date even before going to debrief George, the managing partner, on how the meeting had gone. He came to an abrupt halt by her empty chair. Damn. He looked around, encountering Gina's bland look.

'She's not here,' she said.

Disappointment hit him in the chest and a bad feeling rose with it.

'She's at home. Sick.'

He flinched, the bad feeling bang on. 'What's wrong?'

'Flu, I think. She sounded terrible.' Gina and Hugo were both watching him closely. Did they know something of what was going on with him and Lissa? Frankly he didn't care what they thought, but he knew Lissa did.

'Right,' he said. 'I just wanted to let her know how we got on today.'

Hugo nodded and went back to his work. Rory glanced at

Gina. Her sceptical 'yeah, right' expression let him know he hadn't fooled her one iota. He winked and left.

An hour and a bit later, after meeting George with James and Marnie and wangling the afternoon off as time in lieu, he was bounding up another flight of stairs. Thank God he'd driven her home that night otherwise he'd have had to con her address out of Gina or HR. That would have definitely raised eyebrows.

He reached the door of her flat and pounded on it. If she was sick, he'd take care of her.

Hell.

He'd do anything for this woman.

He stopped banging as he absorbed that idea. Anything?

No, he'd do the same for anybody who was unwell. Compassion, a normal human reaction. He wasn't driven by any greater urgency just because it was Lissa, was he?

He hadn't had a serious girlfriend in a while, didn't want one. Had dated, sure, but nothing much more. He'd been too preoccupied with his career. Damn it, he was still preoccupied with his career. Only now something else demanded his attention.

Lissa.

After waiting a while he rapped again, harder this time, unable to stop the drive that insisted he see her. Finally, he heard some movement on the other side of the door. It opened a fraction and when he saw her big tawny eyes staring at him in surprise, he pushed it right open.

She was wearing an old white tee shirt over panties and nothing else. At least he hoped she wore panties; the shirt hung down to mid-thigh and he couldn't quite tell. All the blood in his body headed south—fast. He forced his eyes back up.

A sheen of sweat bathed her face and her eyes looked huge in her pale face. Huge and slightly glazed. She'd twisted her hair back into a loose, low pony-tail but large sections were escaping.

He thought she looked beautiful, but while his gut twisted with desire he could see she was in no way up to a marathon session of love-making. She looked about ready to collapse on the spot. The protective male bit in him reared its head.

'What?' She looked stunned to see him.

'I wanted to make sure you were OK.' Well, he wanted that and a few other things, but they'd have to wait right now.

'I'm fine.' She leant back against the wall for support.

'No, you're not,' he said softly, stepping into the tiny hall and closing the door behind him.

She pulled upright with visible effort and walked through into the main room. Rory followed, looking about him with growing concern. The place was tiny. A studio apartment and freezing to boot. His concern leapt into worry and then manifested as irritation. He couldn't help but notice the big bed in the corner with the sheets in disarray. He looked away hurriedly. She obviously wasn't sleeping too good, judging by the way the covers were tossed about. Either that or she never made her bed.

'Have you eaten?' He tried to focus back to the basics.

She shook her head weakly.

'Drunk anything?'

Again she shook her head.

His voice rose in irritation. 'Taken any medication?'

She put up a hand. 'Don't start lecturing me. I'm fine; it's just a wee bug.'

He stood back watching as she tottered back to the bed, obviously trying to control the shivering. 'Like hell it's a wee bug. You look half dead.' He swung around the room. 'Where's the kitchen in this place?'

She gestured to the bi-folding cupboard doors in the far corner. He wrenched them open and stared in disbelief. The kitchen, or kitchenette he supposed it would be called, consisted of a bar fridge, a shelf for groceries, about three plates and assorted mismatched cutlery, a microwave, twin hotplate and sink. He looked at the few packets on the shelf. Cereal, cereal and more cereal. All quarter to half full. He opened the fridge, already knowing what he'd find.

Just as he'd thought; skimmed milk and a couple of tubs of yoghurt. The bottle of chocolate sauce standing alone on the middle shelf diverted him momentarily. Wrenching his mind away from the extremely exciting vision of licking chocolate off her breasts, he slammed the door shut with force. 'This is ridiculous. What do you eat?'

'There's a supermarket just around the corner,' she replied defensively. 'I haven't been for a couple of days.'

'Obviously. No wonder you're so trim. You're half starved.'

'I eat at the office,' she said resentfully.

'You eat cereal at the office. Don't you eat anything else?'

'I really like soup,' she replied, tilting her chin up, daring him to criticise her.

Resisting the urge to plant a kiss on those upturned lips as he wanted, he rolled his eyes instead. 'When did you last have a decent home-cooked meal?'

'This is my home. I do cook. And it's none of your business.' She flung herself down on the bed and ruined the defiant effect completely by doubling over and coughing. He moved across to her and rubbed her back in gentle wide circles as she hacked away. He could feel her warmth through the thin tee shirt and he tried not to notice that there was no bra strap under it.

A few minutes later she looked up at him with watery eyes and mumbled, 'Rory, I feel awful.'

He sat down next to her and put his arms around her in the age-old gesture of comfort. He felt no resistance as she leaned into his embrace and he continued to rub gently up and down her back. 'I know, beautiful.' He gently pushed her back onto the bed so she was lying down and hastily pulled a rug up to cover her long legs. Her eyes closed and she shivered spasmodically. He watched her closely. She really looked sick. He could feel the frequent bouts of shivering, and her skin was burning up. The cough was nasty. He guessed she had the flu with a chest infection on top of it. Looking around him, he felt frustrated. She couldn't stay here alone like this. In this condition she wasn't capable of looking after herself and she sure as hell wasn't going to be making any trips to the supermarket for supplies in a hurry. He stroked her arms gently. She appeared to have gone to sleep.

Quietly he stood and surveyed the scene critically. She hadn't a lot of possessions, hadn't bothered to make much of a personal mark on the place. Clean and clutter-free, it looked as if what she had could be thrown together reasonably quickly. An assortment of candles sat arranged on a shelf; he could smell their vanilla fragrance even unlit. Next to them leaned a framed photo of a woman who looked as if she could be Lissa's sister. There were no other photos. New Zealand, eh? Beautiful mountains there, good for snowboarding. He smiled.

A huge pile of books stood stacked in two towers by the bed and he glanced at a few titles with interest. Novels, biographies and a few travel guides. A map of London was taped to the wall. A toiletries bag stood neatly on the chest of drawers. The suit she'd worn yesterday lay in a crumpled heap on the floor by the wall, which surprised him. That didn't seem to fit with the way she wore it so creaselessly. He'd thought she'd be fastidious about hanging her clothes up. She must have been feeling terrible when she got in. Frowning, he picked up the skirt and jacket, shook them out a bit and draped them over the back of a chair. He didn't poke into the wardrobe, feeling as if he was intruding enough.

He spun about quickly; he needed to do something about

her. She couldn't stay here alone. He didn't know if she had other friends to call on and in any case she was in no condition to get to them. Besides, if he knew her at all, she wouldn't even if she could. Miss Cool Independence. He did know one thing for sure; she hated admitting a weakness. Well, undoubtedly she'd hate him for what he was about to do, but tough. Sometimes, he figured, you've just got to lie back and let others help you. He grabbed the keys lying on the table and, flipping open his cell phone, strode out of the flat.

She never wanted to wake up. The dream seemed so real and lovely. She floated in a state of bliss. Soft, comfortable, secure. But it hadn't started that way. Someone had been shining a light in her eyes and from a distance she'd heard an unfamiliar voice asking questions, annoying questions that tried to rouse her, made her feel as if she'd been taken hostage by the Spanish Inquisition and she just wanted whoever it was to go away. Then she'd been hot, so hot and dreadfully thirsty. Her mouth had been too dry to be able to swallow and her lips were cracking. Then he'd appeared. He'd cradled her and helped her drink something cool and refreshing. Then he'd moved away and she'd felt so bereft and so alone. She'd called to him. Asked him not to go.

'Not going anywhere, beautiful.'

She'd rested back against him, smiling, her irritated skin feeling soothed against something smooth and soft. At last she'd slept, cocooned in arms that were tender and strong.

She opened her eyes and blinked at the wall lazily. At least her eyeballs didn't hurt quite as much as they had last time she'd used them. When was that? It felt like hours ago. She came to with a rush. Rory. Rory had turned up on her doorstep. She lifted her head off the pillow and looked around her. Where was he now? Wait a second—where was *she*? She stared at the totally unfamiliar room. There was a snowboard leaning up against the wall and a couple of boxes stacked beside it. The curtains were pulled but she could see a chink of pale light through the gap. What time was it?

Then she became aware of regular breathing near her and she turned her head, rolling over onto her back to look properly. Rory, clad in jeans and a tee shirt, was lying on his side beside her, sound asleep. Her heart stopped in her mouth as surprise came and went in a flash. Fascination took hold. She had never seen him so vulnerable. Until now she'd only seen him in suits or corporate casual wear and even though he had that easy charm he always exuded self-assurance, a commanding style. Now, just in jeans and tee, he looked younger, a little less like the boss and more like a sporty hunk. She studied his mouth, the fuller lower lip that curved into such a devastating smile when he was awake. She took in the long dark lashes resting on his cheek, a hint of a shadow on his jaw. Her fingers itched to rub against it. He looked relaxed. It was incredibly appealing.

She really hoped she hadn't got some form of selective amnesia and was unable to remember what should have been the most awesome sex of her life. She wriggled a little experimentally. While her body ached, it wasn't the kind of ache you got after a night of passionate love-making. And he was lying on top of the bed fully clothed. No, somehow she'd got to his place and he'd looked after her. She remembered her dream, and knew him helping her drink had been real. Guilty pleasure swamped her. She shouldn't be here, this shouldn't have happened, and yet she was so pleased it had. She glanced around the room again with more interest now she knew it was his. There wasn't a lot to make it personal—just the snowboard hinting at athletic pastimes and boxes signalling the recent return from his time overseas. The walls were painted a warm creamy colour and she wondered what the rest of the place was like.

Then she looked under the bedclothes and made a shocking discovery.

'*What* am I wearing?' she screeched.

Rory jerked awake. 'What?'

She watched as alertness sprang into his features and repeated the question.

He frowned as her words sank in. 'Oh,' he mumbled. Then as she watched, amazed, an embarrassed flush mounted in his cheeks. 'You were h-h-hot and sweating.' He was actually stammering. He cleared his throat. 'You said the cotton was too rough on your skin. You were aching. You were complaining about the sheets too.'

'I *what*?' Oh, dear God. She was mortified. She remembered feeling hot and uncomfortable. She must have been feverish. What else had she been muttering while in that delirium? She masked her embarrassment with aggression. 'So what—you just happen to have a selection of silk negligees for whoever comes to stay? I assume this is your, your...'

'Spare bedroom. Yes.' He looked directly at her. The flush had receded. 'And, no, I went and bought it especially for you. In fact—' his eyes gleamed '—I bought two.'

Her mouth hung open for a second before she remembered herself and snapped it shut. She said nothing, absorbing the fact that she was wearing nothing, *nothing*, other than a simple, long silk negligee. No lace, no knickers. 'Did I get changed myself?'

He started to colour again and looked away.

'I didn't think so,' she muttered darkly. Then a coughing fit took over.

'Hey, you're OK here.' His low comment did nothing to soothe her.

She sat up sharply, knowing damn well she wasn't, and the room spun horribly. She wasn't OK and it wasn't the flu bugging her.

'Take it easy,' he said, pushing her back down with a gentle but firm hand on her shoulder. 'You've been very sick and you haven't eaten in days.' His hand lingered. His warm fingers on her bare skin were heavenly. She realised she was hungry. And not just for food.

'What time is it?' she asked abruptly.

He checked his watch. 'Seven p.m. Saturday.'

'You mean Friday.'

'No, I mean Saturday. You've been out of it for over twenty-four hours. You've had me damn worried. But I think half of it was just exhaustion. Once the fever broke, you slept like a child.'

Saturday.

'You want to use the phone at all? Will anyone be wondering where you are?'

She ignored the question in his eyes and simply shook her head. No, if friends called they'd probably think she was out with someone else.

He seemed to have forgotten his hand still rested on her shoulder, his thumb smoothing over her skin. The touch did crazy things to her insides. She shivered and this time it wasn't the fever causing it.

He frowned. 'You lie still and just relax. I'm going to get some food.'

He slid off the bed and she felt sorry as the warmth and weight of him disappeared. She cringed at the hazy memory of begging him to stay with her. What else had she let slip? But she couldn't stop watching him leave the room, his butt shown off beautifully in the low-slung jeans.

She bit her lip and looked up at the ceiling. She was in

trouble here. Big trouble. The question was, did she get up
and try to go home now, or did she just give in and let the inevitable happen? She tried sitting up again and slumped back
in a hurry. The inevitable. No contest.

He reappeared twenty minutes later bearing a tray that, she
had to admit, smelt heavenly.

This time, she discovered, she was able to sit up no
problem at all. She propped the pillow up behind her. He
carefully placed the tray across her knees and smiled. Her
heart thumped slowly and she tried to ignore the tenderness
in his actions.

'This is great.' She gazed in pleasure on the laden tray
before her. In the centre was a bowl of rich red soup accom-
panied by a plate of fingers of buttered toast. A smaller bowl
of freshly cut fruit was also on the tray; it included, of all
things, raspberries. She was in heaven. She picked up the
glass of juice on the side and tasted. Pineapple. How did this
guy know all her favourites? The question must have been
written all over her face.

'You were begging for it last night.' He grinned. 'I had to
go to the twenty-four-hour shop to get it.'

'Thank you.' She put the glass down, having drained half
of it. She felt bad for having reacted so ungratefully before.
'I've put you to a lot of trouble.'

'No trouble,' he said easily. 'Eat your soup—roasted red
pepper.'

She didn't need to be told twice. But while she was hungry,
she wasn't hungry for a huge amount of anything much and
this platter was exactly what she would have chosen herself.
'What about you?' she asked between mouthfuls.

'I ate earlier,' he replied, settling down on the end of the bed.

She couldn't manage to eat it all, but when she finally sat

back she felt a million times better. He smiled at her. She wished he wouldn't; every time he did her resolve disappeared another inch—make that mile.

'Now you need these.' He shook a pill bottle at her.

She frowned.

'Antibiotics,' he explained. 'You have a chest infection as well as the flu. The doctor prescribed these to clear it. So far you've been good about taking them.'

'Doctor? What doctor?'

He grinned at her. 'One of my mates is a GP. He came round after work yesterday and gave you the once-over.'

That explained the man from the Spanish Inquisition.

'You were that worried about me?' She took the dose and washed it down with the remainder of the pineapple juice.

'I was.' He smiled, the warmth lightening the atmosphere. 'Want to stretch your legs?'

She did. She definitely did—stretch them all the way home, or so she ought.

'Do you have something that I can put over the top of... um...' Her voice trailed away and she gestured towards her breast with her hand. She saw the flare in his eyes as he followed the movement of her hands and hurriedly put her arms in front of her breasts to try to hide the all too pleasurable reaction there.

'There was a matching robe.' He stood and went to the chest of drawers, pulling a long cream-coloured silk robe off the top. 'I'll see you in the lounge. You can't get lost.' And he swiftly exited the room.

Bit late for modesty now, she thought ruefully as she swung her legs out of the bed. Still, who was she to be concerned about modesty? If she remembered right she was the one who had been on the desk, begging him to screw her in the middle of the office when people had been due back any minute. Had she no shame? Nope, she realised. Not when it came to Rory.

She sat on the bed for a few seconds, making sure she had her strength together before standing. She was still weak and, underneath it all, still tired. But she didn't want to be lying in bed with Rory lounging on the end of it. That was just too much in the way of temptation.

She pulled the robe around her and glanced in the mirror hanging on the far wall. Her pallor surprised her. And her hair was a mess. She grimaced. What she really needed was a shower. Leaving the room, she discovered Rory was right; she couldn't get lost. Following the sounds of activity, she passed another door—open, showing the bathroom—and another closed; she guessed it must be his bedroom. She quelled the desire to open it and take a peek.

He was in the kitchen, holding two large towels in his hand. The guy really was a mind-reader. 'Want to have a shower? You'll feel better.'

She stopped in front of him and stared. He really did look incredible in those close-fitting jeans and tee shirt. His chest just about took up all her vision, it was so broad. Two towels— one each? Where had her self-control gone?

'Thank you.' Her voice was husky. Her body was starting to feel all sensitive again and this time it wasn't because of the fever.

Slowly he held them out to her, his eyes fixed on hers. Her heart thudded faster. She reached out and took them and looked away from him in a hurry. She had to get out of here or there would be no stopping things. 'I should go home after. Could you give me a lift?'

'You're not going home tonight.'

She'd known he was going to say that. She was also aware she wasn't going to fight him. Much. 'Why not?'

'It's getting late. You're still weak. That flat of yours is freezing.' He'd obviously been storing up a few reasons.

'I forgot to switch on the radiator,' she broke in.

'You're staying here.' They stared at each other. His mouth curved into a wry smile and his eyes twinkled. 'Don't worry. You'll be quite safe.'

Yeah, right. It wasn't him she was worried about. It was her own weak, needy self.

'I'll get that other negligee for you,' he said quietly. 'I'll leave it in your room. I grabbed your toiletries bag from your flat; hopefully it has everything you need in it. It's in the bathroom. I didn't want to pry so I got a toothbrush and comb from the shop just in case.'

'Gee, you've thought of everything,' she said sarcastically, still fidgeting with the belt on the robe. 'Do you do this often?'

He laughed, that open, warm sound that had had her melting on the night she'd first met him. 'No. Pretty much everything with you is a first.'

She wondered what he meant by that.

She headed for the bathroom pronto.

Just as he'd said, her toiletries bag sat on the vanity. She peered inside it. She always had it pretty well packed—just in case she was hit by a sudden urge to take a weekend mini-break. Just beneath her body spray rested her pill packet. She picked it up. She didn't take them for contraceptive purposes, having not been involved with anyone since Grant. The little plastic bubble marked Saturday was full. It was still Saturday. She popped it from the foil and quickly swallowed it. A girl could never be too careful.

Stepping into the shower she turned the taps on hot. The pressure was marvellous and she couldn't resist standing there for long moments letting the water pound on her head and body. It felt so good to get rid of the sweat. She tried not to think about him. Tried to ignore the desire swirling in her belly. It was like trying to stop a tidal wave with a flannel. They were alone. The outside world had disappeared at the door. Just her and Rory. Out of the office and in his home. And she knew and she wanted it to be just so, just for now. She reached for the shower gel—the packaging advertised its therapeutic powers—'invigorate'. She flipped the lid and caught a whiff of the lemony citrus flavour that she associated with him. The gel lacked the underlying masculine tang that was pure Rory but it was close enough. She closed her eyes as she washed indulging in the feeling she was being enveloped by his presence.

He knocked softly on the door as she towelled dry. 'Lissa, are you OK?'

'Fine, I'll be out in a tick.'

Clad in the second negligee—the same as the first only in a pretty pastel blue—and the robe, she padded back out to the lounge. The flat was marvellously warm. Even her feet, which were usually like blocks of ice, were cosy despite being bare.

He knelt, fiddling with the gas fire. 'Sorry,' he said, obviously hearing her arrival. 'You were a while and I was worried maybe you'd collapsed in the shower or something.'

'No.' She grinned. 'It's a girl thing. We take our time in the shower. You guys are all the same. Turn it on, jump in, jump out, get dressed without drying properly and it's all over.'

'Really?' He raised his brows. 'And how do you know so much about it?'

'Flatmates arguing over the power bill.' She smiled teasingly and pulled the robe tighter. She had to admit she loved the silky feel against her skin. Smooth and sensual. Its simple design clung to her; she liked the soft rustle as she moved. She knew it had probably been outrageously expensive. It made her feel sexy. She couldn't help but have sex on her mind. She realised she'd been staring at his jeans-clad thighs. The denim showed off their strong, muscular outline better than his suit trousers. She looked up with a start. She was so aware of him.

'Could I get that comb? I didn't have one in my bag.' Her voice wobbled a bit.

'Sure. I'll go get it.'

She expelled the pent-up air from her lungs as he left the room briefly. But her blood started zinging again the instant he returned, comb in hand. Her fingers brushed his as she took it from him. The sensation from that slightest of touches was enough to send a tremble through her. In the hour and a half since she'd woken up her body's awareness of him had been growing stronger and stronger. Now just the sight of him and the tiniest touch had her craving more. Her breathing shallowed. It was madness to have agreed to stay. But it was a madness she couldn't stop.

She sat on the sofa and tried to comb her hair. After just a few seconds she felt exhausted from holding her arms up. It was pathetic. He seemed to know. She wondered if he knew everything, if he knew how turned on she was feeling, that his nearness drove her crazy. That he was so damn sexy that she just wanted to reach out and plant her mouth on his. Hard.

'Here, let me,' he said in a low tone. He took the comb from her nerveless hand. She turned away from him so she sat sideways on the sofa. He tucked the towel around her shoulders and carefully lifted her hair over it. With long, sure strokes he worked the comb through. The regular rhythm was soothing. Detangling and smoothing.

He stopped and she heard the click as he set the comb on the table. She felt him press the towel on her hair, sponging up the damp. Then he slid the towel away. She sat still, half holding her breath. He seemed to have paused too. And then, just when she knew it would happen, she felt his warm lips on her neck.

CHAPTER SIX

SHE could have stopped what was happening so easily. A look, a word, was all it would have taken. But she said nothing. Her eyes closed, she tilted her head, inviting Rory's kisses to continue. They did. Slow, gentle, incredibly erotic, his lips inched down her neck. At the junction where neck met shoulder his teeth bit down gently.

A soft moan escaped her and his arms slid round to embrace her. One arm encircled her waist firmly, the other seeking her breast. He caressed her, his thumb stroking around her tight nipple. She leaned back into him. This was what she wanted, more than anything. All her concerns started slipping from her mind. Besides, she reasoned dreamily, they weren't in the office, were they? It was perfect.

His arms tightened around her and he lifted her up, settling her across his knee as he sat back against the sofa.

She looked up at him as he held her loosely. She could feel his erection pressing against her side. She knew he was waiting for her reaction, giving her the chance to pull away. Slowly and deliberately she licked her lips. 'Kiss me,' she whispered, her voice wobbling with the force of the need she felt.

Just as slowly and deliberately he lowered his head. She held hers up, in perfect position. The gentle graze of his lips against hers set her nerve ends trembling. She immediately opened her mouth for more and just as quickly he came back with it. Kisses between them could never be small and gentle for long. Their banked-up passion was too strong to be contained.

She felt as if she could keep on kissing him for hours. Long deep kisses in which she finally had the freedom to explore his beautiful mouth, feel him enter hers and make his claim. But slowly, inexorably, the feeling that it wasn't enough soared. She wanted more. She moved restlessly. His hands began a deeper exploration of her body. He loosened her robe and pushed it off her shoulders. The thin straps of the negligee followed. She lifted her arms free of them and the soft material slid to her middle, revealing her breasts. With a groan he quickly lowered his head and fastened onto the nearest nipple. Alternately licking and sucking, he created the most exquisite sensations. She watched him through half-closed eyes, turned on even more by the look of intense pleasure on his face.

His fingers trailed up and down her leg, going higher with each sweep, sliding the silk away so her thighs were exposed. Such delicious torment that she squirmed and her legs parted. Finally his hand hit the top of her thigh and slid against her warm, wet groove. She groaned in delight. That was what she wanted, more, more, more.

He lifted his head and smiled at her. 'You like that?'

Like wasn't the word. She rocked against his hand. He obeyed her silent order and started a slow, rhythmic stroke. She smiled back at him and pulled his head to hers, wanting to taste him again, feel him with every inch of her body. He trailed kisses over her face, down her throat and over her breasts again before passionately returning upwards to her lips and then beginning again until her face and torso were on fire, and she panted helplessly, unable to move, unable to do anything but revel in the sheer, blissful torture of his touch. His fingers gently circled and stroked until she was slick with moisture and rotating her pelvis against his teasing hand. He muttered softly between kisses. 'I want to see you come. I want to feel it, taste it. I want to hear you. Come alive for me, beautiful. Come for me.'

It didn't take long. His words, his lips, his hands, his fingers drove her wild.

'Rory,' she gasped. 'Rory, I want...' she gasped again, unable to get the words out. Not sure what they were any more. Relentlessly his mouth and fingers drove on, not giving her any respite. Her feet arched and her toes curled as the first shudder ripped through her. Still he worked, sucking, stroking, squeezing. Her body arched uncontrollably again and again as sensation zinged through every cell. He pulled the cry of ecstasy from her with ease.

She stilled. Shocked. Her mind refusing to function. Having felt only ache for the last few days, her body wallowed in the weightless warmth now spreading through. She couldn't have opened her eyes if she'd tried. She was vaguely aware of his hand gently stroking her arm, her legs, of being held closely to him. A small part of her whispered for more, that there was more to come, but she wasn't able to focus. Her consciousness floated away.

It was dark when she woke but the room was partially lit with light coming from the hallway through the open door. She blinked, her eyes adjusting to the dimness, her brain reliving what had happened when she'd last been awake. Oh, boy. Aroused again in seconds, she hungered for the main course. He lay next to her, his arm resting on her hip. He breathed evenly but she knew he was awake. She could feel the vitality emanating from him.

She smiled into the darkness. 'Where am I?'

'Where you belong.' His low growl was immediate.

Her stomach swooped. Her pulse stepped up a gear. 'And where's that?' Knowing the answer but wanting to hear it. Wanting to hear the passion in his voice.

'In my bed.'

A rush of satisfaction pooled in her belly. It merged with desire and she pulled his head to hers, fixing her mouth to his, and passionately tongued him. Nothing else mattered. Nothing but being with him in this moment.

She pressed her body length to length against his and elation filled her as she discovered he was gloriously naked. Hot, hard, huge and finally hers.

She pulled her head back and challenged him. 'Where's my negligee?'

She saw the flash of white as he smiled. 'It slipped off.'

'You got a thing about stripping me while I'm asleep?'

She felt his hot breath on her as he chuckled. She explored his chest with her fingers, tracing through the hair. She revelled in the feeling of his hard thighs pressing against her. She longed to run her hands over those too and burrowed a little in the bed so she could.

'I'm sorry I went to sleep on you.' Her voice was slightly muffled. Her hands crossed over his taut abs and down. She found his nipple with her tongue and worked around it, swirling and tasting.

'I'm not. It was beautiful. You're beautiful.' He smoothed a hand down her back.

'I'm awake now,' she said as she reached the top of his thighs with both palms.

'No kidding.' He seemed to struggle to get the words out.

Pleased and emboldened by the night, she took him in her hand. She'd only stroked him a couple of times, appreciating

his length and girth, when he stopped her, his hand gripping
her wrist like a vice.

'Inside you,' he muttered hoarsely. 'I want to come inside
you.' He pulled her back up the bed and kissed her long and
hard and deep and when he finally lifted his head she knew
she was lost.

'Then what are you waiting for?'

He growled with laughter and she melted more.

'I've been waiting too long for this to have it over in two
minutes.'

Oh. Excitement trammelled through her, an almost nervous
anticipation. She didn't know if she could handle much more.
She wanted him now. It seemed as if she'd wanted him for
ever. But he was relentless. His hands, his mouth, slowly,
reverently, traced her body, igniting tiny fires all over that built
and merged and threatened to overwhelm her reason. He
tossed the bedcovers back, the heat between them keeping
them more than warm enough. She learnt his body as he learnt
hers. She gave free rein to all her desires, to touch him, to kiss
him as she'd dreamed of night after night. But he soon pulled
free of her, groaning as he reclaimed control. Then she could
only lie back and let him caress her in ways she'd blushed
about when fantasising.

He nipped gently at the smooth skin of her inner thighs with
his teeth, then soothed the skin with lush kisses.

'Rory,' she whispered brokenly, 'I can't take any more.'

'Yes, you can, beautiful.' And then he kissed her right
there. His tongue hungrily tasted her sweetness, lashing her
with its length, his mouth fastened onto her, regularly sucking
until her hips arched and her hands fisted into his hair. His
fingers came to tease inside her while his other hand tor-
mented a rock-hard nipple.

Her head thrashed and her body shook as she proved her

point—her mind and body imploded as the sensations he stirred catapulted her into ecstasy.

He pressed slow kisses up her belly. 'Are you still with me?'

The power and intensity of that orgasm had far from satisfied her. It had only worsened the unbearable ache in her womb. She needed him there.

'Make love to me, Rory. Please.'

He stared down at her intently, rigid with desire, and then he kissed her, pressing her head down into the mattress with the force of it. The weight of his body settled onto hers and her excitement level sky-rocketed again. She felt the dampness on his skin and knew he was only just keeping himself in check.

He reached across to the bedside table.

'It's OK,' she said. 'I'm on the pill.'

'OK.' He gulped in a deep breath. 'You're sure? You're sure you're ready for this?'

She was more than sure and she wanted nothing between them. He moved closer and she could concentrate on nothing else but him. Her ears were finely attuned to his roughened breathing and her own shallow pants. She pulled at him to hurry, but he held back, braced above her, fixing her in place with his beautiful burning eyes. Then, as smoothly as a hot knife sliding through butter, he filled her. Oh, boy, did he fill her.

Finally.

It felt so damn good that for a moment her mind blanked completely as the sensation short-circuited her whole system. She realised the moan of bliss had been hers. She opened her eyes and looked up at him with a slow, rapturous smile. His unwavering gaze beat down on her. She saw the wonder and delight she felt mirrored in his face. She flexed her hips up to him a fraction.

His breath hissed between clenched teeth. 'Not yet—' his voice tight '—or it won't be two seconds, let alone two minutes.'

She watched as he fought for control, thrilled that he, like she, had almost been obliterated the instant they had joined together. That he felt the passion for her as strongly as she did him.

Slowly he brought up his hand and stroked her hair, then down to frame her face with fingers that shook slightly. Not taking her eyes from his, she turned a little to press a tiny erotic kiss into his palm. She gave him a saucy grin and saw his serious look lighten in return.

At last he moved. Slowly releasing, then pressing close again. Slow, sure strokes that seemed to break through every barrier she'd thought she'd installed permanently. With every movement he filled her, came further into her, breaking into her heart, becoming part of her. And the thing was, it felt wonderful.

She arched to meet him, length to length, stroke to stroke. She ran her hands down his taut muscles, delighting in the ripple of hardness that greeted her.

Slowly, teasingly, he danced with her, sometimes kissing her, sometimes holding her gaze. She kissed his neck; he kissed her breast. But inevitably the pace increased. So too did the intensity and sheer physicality until at last they were pounding hard together. Over and over they met as one until her mind blanked again as he sent her over the edge. Shuddering, she was just conscious enough to feel his big body spasm as he fiercely gathered her closer, his fingers gripping her to him, roaring as finally he too lost his fight for control.

Sweat-slicked and sated, she slept. Silent in the tight embrace that he'd locked her into once he'd shifted the bulk of his weight off her. Somewhere in the back of her mind the thought niggled that she should be going home. That she should be running, far and fast. But she was tired. So tired. And so content. She would wake, see him, want him, have him and then crash again. She couldn't remember whether that had happened three, four or five times through the night. All she knew was that it still wasn't enough. He was a sex god. She'd never experienced such pleasure. Now that she had, she wanted it again, over and over. Just this night, she told herself, just let me have this one night.

In the morning the magic sanctuary of the darkness remained. It was as if a bubble had descended, enclosing them in a world where only they existed. Where doubts and pasts and futures lay forgotten, forbidden. She sat on one of the bar stools at the kitchen bench in her silk negligee, loving the sight of him pottering in the kitchen wearing nothing but a pair of tent-shaped boxers. There was something so decadent about the scene. He cooked her soft, creamy eggs that slipped down her throat. She beamed at him, ignoring the fact that the strap of her negligee had slipped from her shoulder and she was dangerously close to flashing him. When had anyone cooked for her last? When had anyone made her feel so cared for? So cosseted? So *loved?*

Her smile died as she stared at him, her breakfast abandoned. This couldn't be love. This was just attraction. That was all it could be. He held her gaze as he tossed the pan aside and came to her, his eyes lancing, exposing her doubt. Then he bent his head and with only a few gentle touches made her forget. Forget her concern, forget her rules, forget the egg. She went up in flames. Hard and fast with her perched on the edge of the bench, him standing before her. Her negligee rucked up, his boxers halfway down his muscular thighs. Then he suddenly scooped her off the edge and took her weight himself, deeper, harder, joyous. It was as if he wanted to support all of her himself, be the foundation from which she could fly.

She leaned against him in recovery, breathing hard like

him, still overwhelmed by the tornado-like climax they'd
shared. He cradled her for long moments, the after-play of his
hands soothing her, keeping the devils at bay.

He picked her up again and carried her to the bathroom.
Stood with her under the hot shower, soaping her back, mas-
saging her shoulders. Invigorating was definitely the word for
his showers. He aroused her again, slower this time, but no
less passionately.

She slipped into the robe knowing she ought to be pulling
clothes on instead. But the tiredness controlled her and she
pushed the thoughts away, tried to turn the mute button on the
doubts whispering at her. *What are you doing? You shouldn't
be here. You're making a fool of yourself—he'll make a fool
of you...* She pressed the mute button again. It worked that
time. He bundled her up in a soft mohair blanket on the sofa,
put a selection of books on the floor beside her and a jug of
water. His ministrations were so tender and caring she was
afraid to read the motive that lay behind them. No one had
cared for her like this, not since her mother had died. Weakly
she closed her eyes, blocking out the significance. Seconds
later she fell asleep.

'Lissa we need to talk.' The sofa had sunk under his weight
as soon as her eyes had opened.

'No, we don't, Rory.'

'I think we do.'

'No.' She looked at him firmly. She didn't want this, not
now. She just wanted to feel. Just wanted to prolong the magic
a little longer before she had to end it for her own protection.

His eyes were full of the unspoken. She allowed herself to
indulge for a moment. But those doubts came rushing in. Was
this going to be the talk where he made promises? Promises
of the kind that Grant had made? As her mother's boss had

made to her? Insincere? Meaningless? She couldn't trust him.
After all, she barely knew him. The weak part of her
rebelled—she did know him. She'd witnessed his integrity at
work, his drive, his charm. She was in his apartment, for
goodness' sake, something that had never happened with
Grant. There certainly was no sign of another woman's
presence in his life.

No. She had to believe this was just a brief moment. A
fling. Once she went home, it would be over. She could never
have a relationship like this in the office.

She knew he watched her intently as she thought. 'Lissa…'

Unwilling to listen to what she thought would be lies and
too afraid to take the chance they weren't, she moved quickly
to silence him, literally swallowing his words.

Later he went back to the kitchen, bringing her more soup.
They ate leisurely and had each other for dessert.

At one point she woke, her body aching but sated. Her
head rested on his thigh as he sat at one end of the sofa and
she lay along it. Music softly played as he read. A great wave
of tenderness bathed her. He was gorgeous. Such a generous
lover. She wanted to do something just for him. She smiled a
small secret smile. Who was she kidding? She wanted to do
it for herself, while she could. She rolled over so she was
facing into his body, his crotch in front of her. Before he could
stop her she undid his jeans and freed him. He was rock-hard
in seconds. She took him in a firm grip, squeezing slightly.

'Lissa?'

She loved the husky note in his voice. She shushed him.
'Just let me.' She leaned forward and began her oral exploration. She heard his book thud on the floor. Then she was
caught in her own pleasure of discovering him. She traced the
ridge of him with her tongue, closed her eyes and breathed in
his maleness. Nuzzling, stroking, she loved the pulsing she

felt in response. Her awareness of her surroundings faded completely as she lost herself in the taste, feel and smell of him. With both hands she worked him, keeping him in place as she caressed and kissed and sucked, hot and hard.

'Stop, stop, stop!'

She finally heard his cries. She glanced up at him.

'I'm going to come,' he panted.

She chuckled, her hands continuing to stroke. 'That's the whole point,' and then lowered her lips again and sucked as she would her favourite lollipop. He pulsed and jerked and she revelled in the sound of his harsh groan as he gave her all he had. She loved the power of reducing him to merely a body capable of nothing but enjoying mindless pleasure, the power he had over her. A weekend of physical pleasure, that was all it was, all it could be—right?

Licking her lips, she looked up at him with a satisfied smile. 'I'm sure it's good for me.'

'I *know* it's good for me.' His face was flushed and he breathed hard. 'You're going to give me a heart attack if you do that again.'

She pouted.

'Just warn me next time so I can be ready,' he explained.

'You're always ready.' She slapped at his chest playfully. 'That's what I like about you.'

She yawned and stretched her toes. Turned again and re-settled her head comfortably on his lap. Her eyes drifted shut. Warm and snug by the fire, cocooned in his arms, she'd never felt so content.

His amused voice seemed to come from miles away. 'I thought I was supposed to be the one who rolled over and went to sleep.'

CHAPTER SEVEN

SHE kept the mute button on those damn alarm bells that kept trying to ring off in her head. As the day dragged into evening neither of them raised the subject of her going home, or work, or what was happening between them. After she'd stopped his attempt earlier it was as if they had an unspoken agreement to ignore it completely and just enjoy the now.

She knew she should leave, that staying meant it was only going to be harder tomorrow, but she was still so damn tired and it wasn't just her body fighting fatigue, but her will as well. She just couldn't deny it any more. Her desire for him was overwhelming. And now she had known the fulfilment of it she couldn't seem to give it up. She just wanted to give into it over and over. One more night, she promised herself as he pulled her to him, just one more night. But the mute button was failing so she tried mental earmuffs. Ten seconds into his kiss she was in the clear, her mind latched onto one thing only.

The loud beeping of his alarm startled her.

'Damn,' he groaned. 'I have to go.' But he made no move to leave the bed; rather he proceeded to awaken her fully with his own playful style.

He wandered off to shower and, appalled, she felt the

lethargy return. As she lay recovering she broached the subject she'd been ignoring for the last thirty-six hours.

'I should go home and go to work.' She said it as soon as he walked back into the room.

'No. You're still sick.'

She half drowned his reply as she hacked through another coughing fit. Holding his shirt, he looked at her with the most outrageous 'I told you so' smirk.

She sighed, her eyes watering. 'I should at least be recovering at home. The fever has gone.'

'No.' The finality in his tone was unmistakable. No doubt about it. He was used to getting what he wanted. Getting used to having her. Trouble. Ignoring the fact that what he wanted from her was exactly what she wanted from him, she forced irritation to the fore.

'Rory,' she began crossly, 'I can't stay here.'

He leaned over her, his arms imprisoning her in the bed. He kissed her slowly. 'You can't go. You've got no money, no clothes, and I've got your keys.' The devilish glint in his eye softened. 'Just get some sleep, beautiful. We'll talk tonight, OK?'

Incredibly she did spend most of the morning asleep. The cough still racked and her body felt as if it had been hit by a bus. Not surprising given the workout it had had in the last two days. She smiled. Rory had amazing stamina.

She scavenged in the kitchen for brunch and realised she was looking forward to him walking through the door. Counting the hours, in fact. Uh-oh. The phone rang and she stared at it, holding the fridge door open although it wasn't that causing the chill on her skin. It clicked to the answering machine.

'It's me. Pick up.'

Rory. She picked it up immediately, instinct overriding

better judgment. It was a brief call; he seemingly had nothing of great importance to say. She was certain he'd only called because he'd wanted to make sure she was still there.

'I'll be home as soon as I can.' He rang off.

Home.

She slowly put the phone back on its cradle and stood staring at it for long moments. Where was home? She had been travelling for almost two years loving every moment. But her time was up. Her ticket already booked. She had friends she hadn't seen in all that time already planning lunch dates. She was looking forward to it, damn it. The old saying popped into her head, mocking her. 'Home is where the heart is.' Tears sprang at her eyes. She knew just where her heart was— in trouble.

She leaned against the bench for support as she began to realise the full consequences of what she had done. She'd tried to stay away from him because she knew how dangerous office affairs could be. But she'd succumbed to the attraction in the privacy of his home. And in doing so she'd opened herself up to a far greater hurt. Even if she did think for a moment, just for a moment, that he was as crazy about her as she was for him, it still wasn't going to work because her flight was booked. She was going to have to say goodbye to him. And as hard as that would be it would only get worse the more time she spent with him now. Saying goodbye sooner would be better than later.

Her mother had suffered years of loneliness and heartache after the death of her lover, Lissa's father. He'd died when Lissa was only a tiny life growing inside her and her mother had been little more than a child herself at the time. To lose a lover, your true love, be it through death or geographical circumstance, was devastating.

The force of her emotion terrified her and she knew in her

bones it was only going to deepen further. She'd really fallen in love with him. He had his career here, his family, his life. Even if he wanted to she wouldn't let him give that up. Besides, this was just an affair for him. Who was to say it was anything more than a weekend's 'distraction'?

Doubts raced at her, scurrying through her mind, making her feel fear, making her want to run. She tried to fight it.

She went back through to the lounge and stared half-heartedly at the bookcase. She needed something to read for a while. Daytime TV depressed her and if she went back to bed now she wouldn't get a wink of sleep tonight. Then again, maybe that wasn't such a bad idea—a night of insomnia with Rory for company? Bad idea. She shook herself; she had to get this under control.

She stared at the spines of the books, uninspired. And then she saw the album on the bottom shelf. Guiltily, knowing she shouldn't but unable to stop, she pulled it towards her and opened it. Rory the gorgeous as a baby, aged two, and onwards till it ended with him looking about sixteen. She turned the pages, entranced at the images of him. Amazed that the features she adored had been so noticeable from such a young age. Those vivid green eyes, and thick dark hair. She traced the development of his strong male physique. No boy should have shoulders so broad. She half laughed at the awful clothing he'd worn as a young teenager, knowing she'd been as guilty of the same crime. She studied the pictures of him with his parents and sister. They looked a close family. A happy family. It was obvious they still were—devoted Uncle Rory. She sighed and looked across at the fire, gloomily pushing away the spark of envy. They were poles apart. How could they ever have a future together when their pasts were so different? She'd had only her mother, her father dying before she was born, her grandparents had rejected both her mother and her. After her mother had been killed in an accident she'd been alone and naïve and fallen for Grant. She seemed destined to make this kind of mistake.

Game over. She paced, ready for him. She'd been wearing a groove in the rug half the afternoon, going stir crazy. Getting incredibly anxious about the mess she'd got herself into with her uninhibited indulgence. She needed to get outside. Most of all, she needed to get away from him. She'd woken from the dream and those alarm bells were ringing non-stop. Nothing she could do would silence them now. It was only a matter of time before he hurt her, intentionally or not. Sure, she'd just had a weekend of the best sex of her life and she loved the way he could make her laugh, but it wasn't going to last and she needed to get out now before she ended up totally wrecked. She had to say thanks, goodbye and move on. Back to work, back to platonic. For a moment she dreaded his reaction—would he turn on her as Grant had? Surely not. But she had a goodbye planned, one she was determined to enjoy.

The key sounded in the lock and she marched over to meet him. She watched as he entered and with bitter-sweet pleasure saw the desire already evident in his face. It grew as he looked her over. She had dressed in a pair of his boxers and a shirt, unbuttoned to the waist. She saw the gleam of anticipation in his eyes.

'Come and sit on the sofa,' she invited softly. 'You must be tired from a hard day.'

'Tired is the last thing I'm feeling,' he replied, but complied anyway, taking a seat in the middle of the sofa.

She looked down at him, a soft smile curving her lips. She watched as an answering smile spread across his features. His eyes twinkled. She loved that lusty, expectant look he got. She loved it that he was hot for her the minute she looked at him. His hand went to loosen his tie.

'Uh-uh,' she said, shaking her head, determined to keep it light, keep it fun.

He stilled and his grin turned wicked.

'OK,' he said. 'You're the boss, huh?'

'Damn straight,' she replied. He certainly was a quick learner, but then she knew that already.

With a fluid movement she peeled off the boxers she was wearing. She moved forward and straddled him on the sofa, her knees comfortable in the soft cushions on either side of him. He rested his head back and watched her as she undid his belt and trousers, pulling them aside just enough to free him.

'You're every fantasy I've ever had, you know that?' he muttered.

She smiled.

'Only more,' he added reverently. 'Much more.'

She touched her mouth to his, protecting herself from those powerful eyes and tempting words.

He was ready and she'd been ready for hours. There didn't seem much point in mucking around. She bent forward and feathered kisses along his jaw.

'I'm going home tonight,' she whispered as her hands slid down, holding him where she wanted him.

His head jerked up. She stopped him replying by placing a finger on his lips and squirming her hips down on him hard. She felt him gasp as she took him into her all the way. Then she leant forward and kissed him ruthlessly. She couldn't block the emotion: desperation and sorrow and all her desire. She held nothing back. Then passion increased and it flooded out the heartache. She longed to give everything to him but she couldn't. All the while her hips moved sinuously against him with a slow and crazy rhythm. When she freed him from the kiss he was panting, his hands hard on her hips trying to control the tempo and pull her even closer.

She tossed her head back. 'I'll stop right now if you don't agree.'

Who was she kidding? She couldn't stop now if she tried, her hips seemed to have taken on a life of their own and she desperately rode him harder. He knew. He bucked upwards and she sucked in her breath, unable to stop the answering rotation of her hips. A lazy grin appeared on his face, but the red tinge in his cheeks gave him away.

'Oh, so you're playing hardball,' he mocked.

'You'll be the one with hard balls if I don't get what I want.' She could do this; she could. It was to be their last time together and it was going to be dynamite.

'I've got what you want and it's right here, beautiful.'

True, but only for a limited time. Doubt gnawed at her. Part of her would love to believe in him, in this. She pushed the thoughts aside and strove for nonchalance; she was not going to ruin this final coupling.

She raised her brows, moving slowly against him. 'Cocky.'

'Very.' He nuzzled against her breast. 'I bet I can make you come before I do.'

She pulled back and looked at him. A smile tugged her lips. 'Well, now, that is a challenge. And the prize?'

'Where you spend tonight.' His hot mouth covered one of her hard nipples and sucked on it hard. The desire to ravish him increased threefold.

'Fine.' She threw her head back as she savoured the tugging sensation at her breast. God, he was good. But she could be too. She flexed her most feminine muscles, hard, several times.

He whistled slightly as he sucked in a sharp breath. His fingers bit into her hips a second before he shifted slightly beneath her. Then he looked up at her and grinned slyly. 'You forget—I'm getting to know you, Lissa. I know what you like.'

She pressed her lips together. That was certainly true. She opened her mouth to breathe out heavily. She needed to regroup, but his attentions were proving hard to ignore. She closed her eyes. What was his thumb doing? Pushing all the right buttons. She moved and tightened again, retaking control. She felt him tense and smiled a little. This was one bet she couldn't afford to lose...

In the finish they tied. It hadn't been a long race either, the pleasure of giving doubling the pleasure of receiving. They lay sprawled on the sofa, him still half dressed, clothes askew, her completely naked and wanton.

Coldness stole into her. She sat up and pulled on his shirt, wrapping it tightly around her. It was finished. It had to be.

'I'm going home tonight, Rory. Even if I have to walk there barefoot and break the window to get in. I'm going home.'

He stared at her moodily.

'You can't have everything your own way,' she continued, looking away from the disappointment she glimpsed in his eyes.

'I want you to stay.'

She jerked her head back. It had sounded suspiciously like a command.

His green irises darkened, drawing her in. 'We have to talk about this.'

She rose from the sofa, turning her back on him, ignoring his frustrated growl. She needed to keep this light. Not enter into a heavy conversation in which declarations might be made. False promises, the rashness of passion. Better to chalk it down to a fun weekend—one to be walked away from. 'What would you have me do—stay here for ever as your sexual playmate?' She glanced over her shoulder at him.

A wolfish grin leapt across his features. 'Not a bad idea.'

She ignored him and started on her arguments. 'I'm going back to work tomorrow. I need to get home and sort my stuff out.'

'I don't think you should. You're still pale, you look exhausted.'

'And who's to blame for that? You think I'm going to get much sleep here?'

'What if I promise not to touch you?'

She threw him a sceptical look. 'Look what happened the last time you promised that. Forty-eight hours later you were ravaging me in the stairwell. I need to get back to work. They'll be getting a temp in to cover for the temp. I want to go, Rory.'

He studied her and she met his gaze squarely. He looked sombre and she knew she had won.

'OK, I'll run you home after dinner.'

'No, I should go now.'

'After dinner.' He spoke abruptly. He looked at her and softened a little. 'I've seen what's in your fridge, remember?'

She decided to quit while ahead.

They barely spoke through the meal. She tried to eat something but her appetite had vanished. She caught him looking at her several times with knowledge in his eyes and, coward-like, she looked away, trying to buy a few minutes' more time before she had it out with him. Despite the frenzied love-making they had just shared her body was starting to ache with want again and she knew she needed to get away from him fast.

They drove across London in silence. His car wasn't too flashy, not a convertible, but big, German and fast with plenty of leg-room. Many women would be wowed. She wasn't. She didn't like thinking of him wowing the ladies as she'd joked that first night. She stared out the window, her mind absently ticking off the sights, her heart, for once, not in it. It was occupied by something else. The big, tall hunk of a man next to her she was determined to reject.

He pulled up in front of the estate. He turned the engine off. She made no effort to move. They sat in silence. Her brain whirred.

Finally he looked at her and sighed. 'Go on, then, say it.'

'Say what?'

'Whatever it is that's been on your mind all evening.'

She stared at him and then focussed ahead on the motor-bike parked outside one of the ground-floor units. He was right, time to say it.

'I wanted to say thank you for being so good to me while I was sick.'

'And?' he prompted. He wasn't making things any easier.

'And I really appreciate it, I do. And I wanted to thank you for…' she faltered as she searched for the words '…for giving me such a great weekend.' She could feel the heat from her blush on her cheeks. This was ridiculous; she sounded like a schoolgirl thanking her best friend's parents for a nice trip to the movies.

'But?' he prompted again.

She grimaced at his ability to pick her mood so easily. 'But I don't think we can continue this any further.'

'What?' he asked.

She turned and looked at him. 'We go back to being work colleagues tomorrow,' she said firmly. 'Nothing more.' The fatal words were uttered and she felt her heart shatter into a million pieces.

CHAPTER EIGHT

INCREDIBLY Rory laughed. He threw his head back and laughed, really hard. 'You're kidding, right?'

Lissa stared at him, shocked.

He sobered and stared back. 'You're serious.' The wonder in his tone did nothing for her confidence. A smile twitched at the corner of his mouth. 'Lissa, don't you get it? It's too late. The volcano's erupted, the dam's burst, the horse has bolted. The genie is out of the bottle—'

'Enough with the clichés.' she interrupted sarcastically.

He carried on, ignoring her. 'There's no going back. We're on a runaway train, darling. There's nothing you can do but hang on for the ride.'

And wait for it to crash? No, thank you. She inhaled deeply and spoke sharply. 'Stop it. Next you'll be talking in management speak. All about low-hanging fruit and synergy.'

'Well, we do have the most amazing synergy.' He sighed. 'Lissa, you can't be serious. We've just had the most incredible weekend together. I know you haven't wanted to talk about it, but you can't deny it. This isn't just anything. This is special. Why can't we enjoy it while it lasts?'

For once it was panic rather than lust speeding up her pulse. 'Rory, it was just great sex.' She stared at the motorcycle. How could she ever have thought this was going to be easy? This was Rory, champion charmer and people manager.

'That's bull and you know it.' He seemed to be going for the less charm, more honest approach. 'We made love, Lissa. Your words. Remember?'

She gulped and tried to ignore the direct hit. She couldn't let it work. 'No, Rory, it finishes. You know you're the same. You never blur the line between your private life and your professionalism.'

'Professionalism?' He swore sharply. 'This is crazy. You're wanting to throw this away on some temp job?'

She clenched her teeth together. The panic receded and anger ran icily through her veins. He thought it was just some temp job, did he?

'Yes, I am,' she said coldly. 'Because that temp job is important to me.'

She saw anger flash in his eyes. 'Don't you think it's just a little too late for this?'

'It's never too late. These things can be contained. It was a fling, Rory, that's all.'

'Really?' His eyes glittered and she realised she'd just made him very, very angry.

Before she could move he'd leaned across and pressed his lips to hers. Not hard and fierce, but gentle and tender. Taken by surprise, she let her guard slip. Her mouth softened and, oh, so skilfully he parted her lips with his tongue, slowly deepening the kiss. It was beautiful. Absurdly she wanted to cling to him. Why did he have to make this so hard? He lifted his head, his eyes still flashing fire.

She looked back at him, willing the silly tears in her own eyes to disappear. The awful tiredness had returned and she just wanted to crawl off into bed. With him, but that was something she could barely admit to herself.

'Why do you want to stop this?' he asked softly, and she closed her eyes against the desire she saw in his and summoned the anger and hurt she'd felt in the past.

'Just because you're my boss at work doesn't mean you can boss me about here. You don't call the shots.'

She heard his sharply indrawn breath. 'Now, hang on, Lissa. It really bothers you, doesn't it? The fact that I'm your boss.'

She clenched her teeth. The whole thing bothered her. How had she let this happen? She beat her head back on the headrest of the car seat.

'Look, if it makes you feel any better I can arrange it so we're not assigned to the same team again. I won't be your direct manager.'

It was like Grant all over again. She couldn't stop the barrage.

'You think that makes it OK? That it's fine that you can re-arrange my career for me? That who I get to work with, or what project I'm on, is down to you. That my work options are limited because of an affair that we're having?' She'd had one boss who had unfairly controlled her employment options. She refused to have another.

'Well, what would you have me do, Lissa?'

'The situation is impossible. It will never work. We stop this thing now.' The anger was all to the fore now; she could ignore the icy pain in her chest.

'So you're telling me that for as long as we're working together we can't *be* together.'

'That's right.'

He stared down at her thoughtfully. 'OK, beautiful, have it your way.' His face had hardened and remoteness replaced the tenderness in his eyes.

She opened the door and stepped out into the chilly night only just catching his low murmur, 'For now.'

She trudged up to her door feeling as if she'd just ripped out her heart, stuck it in a Ziploc bag and shoved it in the bottom of the freezer.

Rory strode down the corridor unable to stand it any longer. He hadn't seen her for two days and it was killing him. He'd purposely avoided the information centre. She obviously needed time to cool off and think about things. Maybe the weekend had been too overwhelming. It sure had blown him away. Maybe they should have talked about things earlier instead of leaving it till that car ride home. But he'd known she hadn't wanted to talk much and, to be honest, nor had he. He'd just wanted to go with the moment and had hoped that every time they'd made love she had sunk deeper into his web as he had hers. Magic—no other word for it. But doubt gnawed at him. For the first time in his life he felt uncertainty. He couldn't see where this was going. Wasn't sure he wanted to. All he knew was that he wasn't ready for it to end. Not yet.

His gut tightened. But what about her? Could she switch off just like that? Maybe it had just been a weekend of wild sex and nothing more. Maybe it *was* all over as far as she was concerned. She pushed him away at every corner.

He thought back to that parting kiss. She'd wanted more then. No, he couldn't believe it was finished, but he needed to know for sure she still wanted him. He stopped off at the Gents on the way to calm down and get a grip. He couldn't exactly just march in, grab her and kiss her senseless even if that was all he wanted to do. He stared at his reflection in the mirror. Something was bugging her. She'd said she didn't like being talked about. That was why her behaviour was usually so circumspect in public. He grinned; she wasn't quite so circumspect when she was dealing with him. In public or private. She couldn't seem to stop herself from reacting to him—teasing him as much as he loved to tease her. He got to her and he needed to play on that for all he was worth.

She hated that they worked together. Hated that he was her boss. He frowned. She hadn't been impressed when he'd suggested he arrange it so they were no longer on the same team. Too late to change things now, but he was sure she'd be pleased when she learnt what had been done. And at least it removed that particular obstacle.

The fact was he wanted to spend more time with Lissa. And not just time in bed. She was beautiful, smart, funny and he loved the way she teased him. He loved the way she laughed at his lame jokes. He found her zest for life intoxicating. She was fun to be around. And then there was the sex. Spectacular. He'd known she was passionate but, flu or not, she was amazing. Every waking moment of that weekend she'd been at him. It made him want to throw his head back and roar like a lion. It made him want to stake his claim big time. He wanted to go exploring with her. He wanted to tag along on her tourist outings. Laugh with her about being ripped off by ice-cream vendors in Italy. He couldn't believe she hadn't been to Florence. He wanted to take her there. Stand with her when she saw Botticelli's Venus for the first time, wink with her in front of Michelangelo's David. Drink wine, eat lots and make love morning, noon and night. It was as if he'd come home to a holiday romance.

His heart beat faster with every step nearer her desk. She was looking magnificent in a red suit, the jacket buttoned up. She'd swept her hair back into a severe style, the golden tresses locked away. He grinned. She looked the *über*-professional ice queen. She would. She didn't look up as he approached. Only when Gina said, 'Hi, Rory,' did her head fly up. He watched her intently. No mistaking the flash of fire in her eyes. She quickly dampened it but he took perverse satisfaction in watching a slow tide of colour rise in her cheeks. An uncomfortable silence prevailed.

'How can we help you?' Gina finally broke it.

He thought about his reply a second, wishing he'd had the nous to actually think up an information request before charging up here.

Lissa suddenly stood. 'I'm going to sort out those CDs,' she muttered.

Rory wasn't sure to whom. She marched down to the other end of the room behind the book stacks to where the search computers were. So she wanted to get away from him did she? Tough. He couldn't help but watch her as she moved. Her red skirt ended just above her knee. He mentally slid a hand under the skirt, imagining the stockings and suspenders he knew he'd find underneath. He drew in a sharp breath and studied the painting on the wall nearest him. Geometric blocks of colour sploshed haphazardly over a white canvas. Thank God. A nude or even a still life with ripe, round fruit would have been a problem. He needed to think neutral thoughts or he'd be in big trouble.

Equilibrium restored, he turned to follow Lissa. He found her viciously shoving CD cases back into their respective shelves.

'You know—' he forced himself to speak lazily '—for someone who wants to avoid attracting gossip, you're going the wrong way about it.'

She didn't look up. 'If you're wanting some information, Gina can help.' Her hands continued sorting the CD-Roms.

'I don't want information.'

She hesitated. 'Then—'

'I want you,' he interrupted. He watched happily as she

stood breathing shortly in front of him. Puffed from handling a few CD cases? No, that was him; this thing between them. Electric. How it had always been. He stepped closer, she didn't move away.

'I missed you.' He spoke honestly. He didn't know what else to do. He saw indecision on her face and offered a smile.

'Rory, please.'

She didn't smile back; if anything she looked more distressed. Then he recognised it—fear.

After a couple of false starts he managed to say the words he hoped would reassure her. The words he meant with all his heart. 'I'm not going to hurt you.'

Her lashes swooped down, hiding her response.

He didn't know if it had been a dumb thing to say. He waited another second, watching the tide of colour in her cheeks flow and then slowly ebb.

She opened her mouth and suddenly he knew he didn't want to hear what she was going to say. He put his fingers on her lips and before he could stop himself he swooped and stole a quick kiss. It blossomed immediately. His heart thundered. He felt her soften and he swore he heard a soft moan escape her. His hand lifted to hold her head to his and he felt her tremble. Hurriedly he pulled back. They would go from naught to two hundred in a nanosecond, but not here.

She stared up at him. He watched as emotions warred within her. He decided to relent for now. He'd found out what he needed to. The rest could wait. She'd come to it soon enough. There was no reason they couldn't be together until she left. They needed to have a big talk, preferably one that ended up in bed, but now was not the time.

He smiled at her. 'That was a freebie. Next time you ask. See you 'round, beautiful.'

He turned and walked away, only just winning the battle not to swing back and take another look at her. It might only be lust, but she couldn't deny that she had feelings for him and those feelings would win out. Rory one, Lissa nil.

Having the most orgasms in her life in a three-day period had the most unfortunate after-effects for Lissa. It was as if now she'd been switched on she couldn't be switched off, walking around in a permanent state of semi-arousal. It took only the slightest friction or most fleeting thought of Rory to result in a flood of heat and the mad desire to go find him, press against him and take him in. She could only be thankful that their two-week period confined in a room was over. There was no way she could hold fast to her resolve if he were in such close proximity. She tried to concentrate on the information request before her, but every time someone entered the information centre she looked up—the original rubberneck.

She tried to blame her struggle for concentration on the after-effects of the flu, but her heart knew better. She kept replaying that morning's all too brief kiss with Rory at the other end of the library. He'd completely ignored her call to end it. He wasn't giving up on her. The knowledge made her giddy. He'd sought her out and proved to her that he could move her. What the hell was she going to do? The fact that they could have been seen by anyone wandering in the library hadn't occurred to him. Maybe the thought of people knowing they were an item didn't bother him. Grant would never have taken such a risk. In a perverse way this pleased her. Here was Rory, the one and only, the guy who never fooled around in the office, messing with her, Lissa, the temp from New Zealand. He'd said he wouldn't hurt her and maybe he genuinely meant it. But he would hurt her, whether he meant to or not. She was already hurting and the only thing she could do now was lessen the severity.

Gina and Lissa logged off simultaneously and called into the bathroom to fix their hair and make-up. Lissa refused to spend these last few weeks moping. She was going to go out tonight, drown her sorrows and resurrect her party spirit. She was going to plan some mini-breaks for her last few weekends and see some of the sights and she was determined to enjoy it. She would not let her flingette with Rory ruin her last weeks of tourism.

Gina turned to face her and shook her hair. 'Am I OK?'

Lissa appraised her. She was wearing a baby-blue pencil skirt teamed with a white roll-neck cashmere sweater that hugged her curves in all the right places. She'd applied a soft pink gloss to her lips and brushed her curly blonde bob so it shone. Her blue eyes sparkled and silver earrings hung from her ears. She shone from the inside out. A petite firecracker. 'You're a doll.'

'Yes, but am I a sexy doll?'

Lissa laughed aloud. 'Absolutely. What about me?' She adopted a mock-model pose for inspection, smoothing her hands down the black silk shirt she'd just changed into and down her slim red skirt. She tossed her freshly loosened hair with a feeble laugh.

Gina rolled her eyes. 'Lissa, you exude sex. You've got legs to your armpits, boobs to match, long golden hair and this haughty 'look but don't touch' façade. Now with this flu thing you're all pale and fragile-looking too. It's a killer combo. You're irresistible.'

'Ha!' Lissa snorted. She knew Gina was over-egging it, but her ego needed the boost and she was happy to receive it.

They quickly walked through the cold rain, sharing Lissa's

umbrella, and climbed the steps leading into the pub. A nauseous feeling rose as the combined smell of beer, wine and perfume met them at the door and Lissa knew the idea of drowning her sorrows was a dumb one. But nor did she go for pineapple juice. Too many memories there. She opted for cranberry, alone and on the rocks.

Lissa was chatting to a young consultant about bungee jumping in New Zealand when Karl made an appearance. He wandered over to Lissa and surprised her completely by snagging her hand and tugging on it. She looked up at him in query. 'What?' she asked.

'Come here, I've got something to show you.' He pulled her over to a quiet corner and turned her so she stood facing the room and he stood with his back to it.

'Jeez, Karl,' Lissa began. 'What's going on?'

His eyes were dancing, but she noted a steely determination shining underneath. He stood with his hands on his hips, and she could feel the pent-up energy within him.

'You're going to do something about Gina?' Lissa asked.

'Uh-huh.' He nodded decisively.

'What?'

'In my book, actions speak louder than words. I'm going to show her how I feel.'

She watched in amused surprise as he undid the top few buttons on his shirt, opening it just enough to reveal the tight tee he wore underneath. Emblazoned across his chest in bold type were the words 'satisfaction guaranteed'. Subtlety wasn't something that Karl did. She looked back up at him and the giggles burst out of her. 'Perfect.' It was as outrageous as he was, as Gina was. The two beautiful flirts were definitely a dream match.

He grinned wickedly back at her, doing the buttons back up. 'I thought so too. Time to make a move.'

'Go get her.' She laughed. 'But, Karl!' He stopped and looked at her. 'Don't forget we chicks need the words too.'

He grinned and saluted and wandered in the direction of the bar. Lissa looked about, trying to spot Gina. She caught sight of her, cornered by a couple of consultants as usual. Lissa watched with satisfaction as Karl approached her. She glanced away and found herself looking at James, who had somehow appeared right in front of her without her noticing.

'What are you doing standing in this dark corner all alone?'

'Oh.' She didn't know what to say and took a quick sip.

'Waiting for someone?' James asked.

'No, I was just talking to someone, but…' She let her voice trail away. James didn't seem overly interested in her reply. He stared at her. She coloured a little, not sure what he wanted. She held her glass in front of her with both hands, hugging it against her body in an unconsciously protective gesture.

'Seems funny to be back at the usual desk, doesn't it? I miss our little team. It was very illuminating.' He paused and looked her over.

Lissa shifted on her feet uncomfortably. She definitely didn't like the way this was heading.

'There's a whole lot more to you than meets the eye. I miss you, Lissa. I liked sitting near you. You're a pleasure to be around, you know that? A pleasure to look at, a pleasure to talk to, and I bet you'd be a pleasure to kiss.'

Whoa, this was too much. The last thing she needed tonight was a charm offensive from James. Hadn't he got the message the last time he'd asked her out? Obviously not. Maybe he thought the two weeks in close quarters with him had made her radically change her assessment of him? She nearly laughed aloud. She'd barely noticed him. She'd felt nothing but awareness of Rory.

Lissa glanced around, half hoping for a saviour. There didn't seem to be anyone near enough to draw into the conversation; most of the crew were over by the bar. She took another sip of her drink. She'd just have to straighten him out. Trouble was, she knew from past experience he was fairly resilient.

'James, I'm sorry, but—'

'But nothing, Lissa. Come on, give me one date. Come to dinner. Get to know me. You might even be pleasantly surprised.' He gave her a charming, overly confident smile that did nothing for her.

Yes, he was persistent, she'd give him that.

She looked over to where Gina had been and saw that Karl had managed to despatch the two consultants who had been loitering earlier. He had Gina alone and both looked serious.

She looked back at James, trying to get him to listen to what she was saying. 'James, I already know you and you're a nice guy, but I'm not interested.'

He frowned. 'You're not interested.' He said it as if there were something wrong with her. 'How come you don't date anyone? Got a murky past?' He moved closer to her, invading her space.

She tensed. How dared he start prying into her personal life? His arrogance astounded her and she felt it time she made herself understood clearly. She was unable to manage polite rebuff, her emotions too on edge. She opened her mouth to give him a piece of her mind when suddenly an arm snaked around her waist and firmly pulled her back against an extremely taut body. Her own body flared and fitted against it perfectly. Rory. She hadn't even seen him approach. His arm reached right around her and his hand spread wide and firm on her lower abdomen. His other hand reached to her shoulder, holding her back against him length to length. A ripple of awareness shivered through her entire body. He couldn't have adopted a more possessive stance if he'd tried. The shock temporarily robbed her of speech.

'She's seeing me, James,' his voice rasped. Lissa felt his anger and her insides melted. He was jealous.

James stood back and looked them over. 'So I see. I wondered about that, but I thought maybe not.' He took a swig of his drink. 'Still, can't blame a man for trying.'

Rory said nothing and Lissa couldn't think of a thing to say either. The uncomfortable silence hung over them, but James didn't take the hint and move off. Rather he looked at them for a few moments. Malice glittered in his eyes.

'Well, Rory, no wonder you had Lissa ditched from the team.' He spoke with a confident swagger. 'Shame for you, Lissa, missing out on the biggest deal Franklin has seen in years, especially when you helped win the contract. Still, now Rory's free to concentrate on the mega project and have you as recreation on the side, while you're stuck doing the filing or something boring back in the library.'

Lissa felt her jaw go slack. What had he just said? She replayed his words. Their meaning sank in. Rory had ditched her from the project? Back to boring library work? So he could have her on the side?

A wave of shock flooded through her. No, no, no. He wouldn't have done that, would he? It was Grant all over again, controlling her career, manipulating her life for his own purposes.

She needed to get away from him. Away from them both. From the whole damn lot of them. She tensed and made to pull away, but Rory's arm was like a steel band pinning her to him. She turned her head to look up at his face, but he held her so close and tight against him all she could see was the clench in his jaw.

She felt the animosity ignite between the two men. They

were like two lions, circling around the kill. She certainly felt as if she'd been mauled. Why would Rory treat her like that? Just so he could keep sleeping with her? Horrified, she felt tears prickle the backs of her eyes and angrily she summoned control. Icy, icy control. She would not be humiliated like this. Not here, not now.

'Things are never quite that simple, James,' Rory said curtly.

James shrugged. 'If you say so.' He gave Lissa a penetrating look, and with a nasty smile he departed.

Rory's arm didn't loosen one iota.

'Let me go.' Her voice dripped with venom.

'We need to talk.' His jaw still clenched tight, ditto his grip.

'I don't think we do. I don't think there's anything to be said.' She clawed at his hand, digging her nails in, not caring at his wince. No way could that scratch hurt him as much as he had just hurt her. He loosened his arm a fraction and she turned in it to face him. Her body still pressed close against his and she was furious with herself for feeling that rush of desire for him when he'd been such a rat. She breathed heavily and with each inhalation her breasts pressed closer against his chest. She was painfully aware of him, of his heat. His magnetism was such a force that even now she was drawn to him. But her heart was breaking and her head filled with a cold furious pain that drove her to repel him.

His rock hard body matched his expression. 'What— you're just going to believe what that jerk said without even hearing what I have to say?'

'Am I off the team?'

'Yes.'

'So we're not working together. You arranged it so you could keep sleeping with me.'

He paused and his eyes flickered.

He had. Used his position as her boss. Exactly what she'd

been afraid of. She pushed both hands against his chest with all her might and broke free. Stepping back, she stared at him, her eyes flashing fire.

He moved after her, lifting a hand to touch her.

She stepped out of reach.

His hand fell. 'Lissa, it's not that simple.'

'I trusted you,' she said lowly.

He frowned. 'This isn't about us, Lissa.'

'There is no us.'

God, would she never learn? Why did she always fall for guys who let her down? Who were all about what they wanted, not caring about her at all. Well, never again. Never, ever again would she let a guy get to her like this. He'd just screwed her over. She turned and headed for the door.

It was impossible to get up much speed through the bar now full of merry patrons. She gave a hurried look over to where Gina and Karl had been but she couldn't see them. She didn't give them a second thought, all she wanted to do was get out of there and lick her wounds.

Maxine from Reception stepped before her, blocking her path. 'What's going on with you and Rory?'

Lissa stopped and stared. She'd forgotten that half the staff had probably been watching their little encounter in the corner and drawing goodness knew what conclusions. 'You really want to know?' she asked shrilly. She wasn't sure quite how it happened, but the noise of the bar had receded completely. There seemed to be nothing but her and Maxine and a constant hum in her own head. Vaguely she saw others turning her way. She couldn't care less. Anger and hurt made her reckless and voluble.

'We had an affair, but it's over now.' Her voice rang clear as a bell. Maxine's eyes widened.

'Wrong, Lissa,' Rory boomed behind her. She spun around furiously to face him. He stood broadly, inches away, legs apart, anger apparent in every muscle. He looked her up and down, raking her body with the heat in his angry glare—a move that only served to enrage her further. Her entire body tensed. It seemed everyone in the room held breath.

'You know damn well it's not over,' his voice drawled through the bar.

For a split second there was total silence. Then there was a collective gasp and a lone wolf whistle.

'Go get her, Rory,' someone yelled.

Lissa stared at him in fury, seeing his pale anger and force of will. And despite it all a trickle of desire was pooling in her belly. She still wanted him. He'd betrayed her and yet her body still wanted to feel his hardness against her.

Disgusted with herself, she turned and ran for it. Pent-up energy gave her speed. Opening the door and flinging down the entrance stairs, she got a good start. The fight-or-flight instinct had kicked in. She was going for both. Her heels tapped as she clattered down the stairs at breakneck speed. She glanced back up. Rory was following three at a time.

'I don't want to talk to you,' she called to him as she started along the footpath. The cold wind bit into her.

'Well, it's about time you bloody did. I want to talk to you.' He advanced closer.

'And it's all about what you want?' she flung back at him. She'd left her umbrella inside and rain was falling in large splats. She increased her pace so she was practically running.

'Lissa, slow down. You'll fall and break an ankle.'

Indignation burned. 'I can run a marathon in these heels.'

'Fine, but not tonight.'

He caught up to her, grabbed her arm and pulled her to a stop. She jerked her arm out of his hand. He stared at her, his jaw clenched. People moved to avoid where they stood in the middle of the footpath.

'Still care about what other people think, Lissa?'

'You know what, Rory?' she yelled in his face, ignoring the interested stares of the passers-by. 'I couldn't care less. What I care about is being used.'

'Finally some honesty,' he yelled back. 'So let's forget about the audience and sort this mess out.'

She hardly heard him as she berated herself, her hands fisting at her chest. 'God, I promised myself I wouldn't do this again. How could I be so trusting and *stupid*?'

He stared at her in silence, waiting for her to continue.

'I should have known you would let me down. It was just a matter of how.' She stood before him, getting wetter as the rain fell, watching as the defence leapt in his eyes and he took breath.

'Lissa, listen to me.' Calm, coaxing.

She closed her eyes and forced her blood to freeze. She would not be manipulated by him.

'What James said wasn't even close to the truth.'

'You wouldn't know what the truth is, Rory. Let alone be able to tell it.'

He flinched, his hands fisted, not quite so calm now. 'Lissa, you're tired and overwrought and being completely irrational.'

'I am not irrational.' No way was she going to let him play the 'you're an irrational female' card. One sign of tears and they thought a woman was all out of control. Typical.

'Yes, you are. You won't even listen to me.'

'It wasn't your place to take advantage of your position. To take advantage of me,' she overrode him furiously.

'I did not take advantage of you and you know it,' he flung back, his voice betraying that he was as angry as she.

She stared back at him. No, he hadn't. She'd been as willing as he had. What a fool she'd been. She'd given in to temptation and lost her heart in the process and now she was paying the price.

'You don't get it, do you? You just organise things the way you want them. I told you we couldn't be together while you were my boss and so you just rearrange my job without any regard to how it might impact on me. Maybe I would have liked the extra hours, maybe the money would have come in handy when I go home. All that matters to you is maintaining your source of hot sex!'

'Lissa, you are so far off base.' The words flew out, demanding her attention. 'The decision was made well before you said that to me, Lissa. George decided last week after the meeting with the client.'

'Last week? George?' She wasn't buying it. He wasn't going to charm his way out of this with his brilliant eyes.

'Lissa, I knew you were gutted about being taken off the Portuguese project; Hugo told me. When debriefing with George the other day it was agreed that, as this project is long-term and the Portuguese is about to wrap, it would be better for Gina to take on the new one and send you back to the other. That way there is better continuity. It was George who suggested it, and George who decided. I just agreed. I think he wanted you to get the Bilbao trip. And I wanted you to have it. I know how much you'll love that gallery.'

She stared at him. Hearing the words. Blinking as they sank in. 'Bilbao?'

'Yes, the weekend bonus, remember?' He glared at her.

Hell, she'd forgotten about it. All disappointment of missing out had been obliterated in the heat and storm of her affair with Rory. Three weeks ago she'd have been moon-walking with delight over the prospect, now it felt hollow.

A raw energy poured off Rory as he continued to enlighten her. 'I think you're just spoiling for a fight and I'm fairly sure I know why. You want to push me away? Fine, but be honest about it. Don't use this as an excuse.' His words whipped, his frustration unmistakable as he stood like a warrior charged and ready for action.

Her shoulders slumped as the fight drained out of her. He was right. She'd been wrong. He hadn't abused his position. In fact he'd been on her side. But it made no difference to their relationship. She was too scared, too hurt and hopeless. Humble pie time. 'I'm sorry for blowing up at you before giving you a chance to explain.'

She stared at him, committing his features to memory; despite the blur of the rain she saw him more sharply in focus than ever before. His height, the dark springy hair and the brilliant eyes that right now were glittering with a fire that had several sources of fuel.

It had to be over. She was leaving. The heartbreak now would be nothing to what it could be. With a final, soft, 'I'm sorry,' she turned and, heedless of the rain or the fact her shoes probably weren't going to make it, started the walk home.

CHAPTER NINE

LISSA had only walked half a block when the black cab pulled alongside her, its engine low as it slowed to keep pace with her. Then it paused just ahead and the door flung open.

'Get in. You want pneumonia or something?'

She stared at Rory as he sat forward, like a jungle cat ready to leap and pounce. His peremptory command was an audible expression of his grim tension. He was still angry. He was still gorgeous.

Her heart thundered, the heat in her body rose, despite the cool, wet air. She hated that she wanted him so much, it just didn't make things any easier. 'Just a ride home.' Utterly unable to resist the order in his eyes, unable to resist her need to spend time with him—even five more minutes.

He shrugged and sat back as she bent to step into the cab.

She perched on the edge of the seat feeling more than a little humiliated. She winced as she recalled the words they had traded in front of the entire bar. 'I'm sorry if I embarrassed you in front of everyone tonight.'

'You didn't embarrass me. I'm happy for the world to know; half the population will be dead jealous. But I admit to being surprised—for someone who once said she wanted private, you picked a hell of a way to go public.'

His gaze slid over the damp blouse clinging to her. She was grateful for her jacket—although unbuttoned, at least it covered her hard and aching nipples. She felt anger at her unrelenting desire for him. His attention then dropped to the edge of her skirt. She pressed her knees together, wanting to stop the excitement. He still looked ferocious, but in a wickedly wanting way. She turned her head to stare out the window, unwilling to look at him. Not wanting to be tempted all over again. *Focus.* 'I don't care what they think, Rory. That wasn't why I said no to you at the start.'

'No.' There was a tiny pause. 'So why did you?'

'I didn't want to get involved with you because we work together, more than that you're my boss, and one thing I learnt the hard way was not to get romantically involved with someone you work with.'

'How learnt the hard way?'

'My mother had an affair with her boss when I was sixteen. She thought she was getting love, marriage, the works. But he was just using her. I last spoke to her as she was driving home after he ended it with her and she lectured me, told me not to make the same mistake. She had the accident five minutes later. Of course, when I was older, I made the same mistake.'

'Fell for your boss?'

She nodded, looking back at him. 'Pathetic, isn't it? My graduate job. He pursued me, flattered me. Told me to keep it a secret from the others because he didn't want me getting flak from them about favouritism. We never went out in public. I didn't really notice or question why—I was just enjoying thinking I had someone. Someone who loved me, who would care for me. I'd been alone for so long. I was so naïve.'

'He was married?'

'About to be. When I finally found out I was horrified. I tried to end it but he got nasty. He started giving me all the donkey work, the boring assignments, harassing me when no one else was around. In the end the easiest thing to do was leave. I'd made the exact mistake my mother had and I vowed not to do it again. Then I met you.'

He looked serious. 'I'm not either of those guys, Lissa. I've always been honest with you and I always will be. There's no one else. You know that. Just you and me.'

The cab had been idling outside her flat for at least five minutes now. She had barely noticed. The air crackled between them. The flames in his eyes still burned. *Just you and me.* She felt the softening deep inside, the want, every cell screaming to get closer to him. The anger and pain of moments before transmuted again into the heat of desire. She tried to force it back.

'It doesn't matter, Rory. It can't continue anyway. I'm leaving the country in less than six weeks. I'm sorry for mucking you around.'

'So you still think it's over?'

'It has to be. It's better to end it now.' Knowing that was the last thing she wanted to do, but how else did she stand a chance of saving what was left of her heart?

'Six weeks is ages.'

Yes. Long enough to cause permanent heart damage. 'It would be a mistake.'

'So that's it, then?' A darkness grew in his expression, one she couldn't read.

'I think that would be best.' She couldn't stop the heat coursing through her body. Here she was arguing with the man, trying to end it with him, and yet her body wasn't listening. It was her body wanting to get closer. Aching for his touch.

She broke the invisible bonds trying to draw her to him, turning quickly away and stepping out of the cab. She heard the door slam shut behind her and, without looking back, she raced up the stairs, desperate to get inside and lock the door behind her for fear she'd change her mind and go after him willing to take any last crumbs in these remaining few weeks like the hopeless case she was.

'Know what I think of that idea?'

She whipped around. Only three paces away Rory strode after her. Glancing over the balcony, she saw the cab driving round the corner, passengerless.

He stopped an inch from her. 'I think it's rubbish.'

Her breath came shorter. 'What do you suggest, then?' She stood beside her front door, unable to get the key into the lock, unable to move, transfixed by the passion in his eyes and the heat in her belly.

'I still want you and I'm pretty sure you still want me.'

The way she couldn't tear her focus from his mouth must have been the give-away.

'One night.' Unable to resist, unable to fight the fire in her body, she capitulated instantly, leaning towards him as she spoke. 'Just one more night.'

'Now.'

'Yes.'

A whisper as the inch of space between them became nothing. No holding back. His kiss was ferocious. She tasted the frustration, anger and want in him. The same frustration, anger and want that she had felt all week.

While still able to, she turned in his arms, forcing the key into the lock and turning it while his arms came around her to rake down her body, pulling her back against him so she felt his tension and rigidity. He stripped her jacket from her shoulders, leaving her damp blouse clinging to her. Waving her arm free of the jacket sleeve, she pushed forward and opened the door. He lifted her from behind and thrust her through the doorway. He stepped after her and had slammed the door behind them before she could take breath. Wheeling in front of her, he pressed her back against the closed door with the full length of his body. She lifted her face and welcomed the hard demands of his mouth, ravishing him with a fierce passion the way he was doing to her. She nipped at his lips with her teeth drawing a vicious thrust from his hips; she panted with pleasure and immediately wanted more. She knew there was going to be nothing slow or leisurely about this merging and nor did she want it that way. She pulled off his tie and fought with his shirt buttons, freeing them and then dragging both shirt and jacket down together so he stood bare-chested against her. He wasn't having the same ease with her blouse and she heard the tear of fabric as in frustration he simply ripped it apart.

With fingers made nimble by sheer will she worked his belt open and his trousers and boxers down, sliding her hands round to hold his butt and urge him closer to her.

He yanked up her skirt so it bunched around her middle and pulled aside the silky strip of her panties with his strong fingers, his erection pressing against her wetness.

He lifted his mouth from hers and for a half-second paused. 'Yes,' she cried. 'Now!'

There were no other preliminaries. With a single, hard thrust he was there and she arched her neck back in abandon. 'Yes!'

She curled her leg around his waist and he immediately hoisted her up so she could wind her other leg around him too. The door and his thighs bore her weight.

His breathing was harsh and ragged as he continued to plunder her lips, her neck, her breasts still confined in their lace scraps. His mouth hot, hungry and unbelievably delightful. He ground into her, deeper, longer. She knew he was as out of control as she'd ever seen him and she wanted it even more.

'Harder,' she incited him, 'harder.'

He pounded against her, inside her, with her and she used her hands, her mouth and teeth to wantonly reciprocate as best she could—alternately nipping, sucking, rocking, driving him to go more powerfully, faster. She raked her hands across his shoulders, down his back, pulling him closer, ever closer. The door rattled on its hinges as she moaned further entreaties for him to show no mercy, loving the wildness of it, until the ferocious and primitive mating resulted in a climax, the noisiest and sweatiest she'd ever experienced.

Utterly lax and sated, she rested against the door, still supported by him. His heart thundered beneath her palm and she used her thumb to brush aside a trickle of sweat from his hair-dappled chest. He'd buried his face in the side of her neck and she felt his hot, laboured breath blowing against her.

'Are you OK? Did I hurt you?' He lifted his head to look at her.

'No. I'm more than OK.' She opened her eyes and smiled at him through lips that were swollen with passion. 'That. Was. Fantastic.' She closed her eyes again, feeling thoroughly replete. For now the devils were well and truly chased away, the stress of the last week physically worked out of her. 'Feel better?'

She heard his sigh. 'Hell, yes. Will be even better when we're curled in bed together.'

'I might need you to carry me there. I don't think I have the energy to move.' Or the will. It was so nice being held by him, still part of him, locked in his arms.

'OK, beautiful. But I need to rest you here for a second. I've still got my shoes on and my trousers round my ankles. If I try to walk we'll both end in a heap on the floor.'

With a half-laugh she unhooked her legs from his waist and he eased her down a little so she could stand. Leaning back, she watched as he quickly kicked off his shoes and stepped from his trousers, leaving them in a dark puddle on the floor together with the rest of the clothes they had managed to remove. Then with a mischievous grin he leant forward and caught her round her middle, swinging her up over his shoulder so she hung upside down over his back.

'Hey, what am I? Your snowboard?'

He laughed. 'Hell, no, you're a lot more fun to ride.'

Her mouth fell open at his cheek and then she realised she was in a perfect position to assess the quality of his other cheeks, and reaching down, she gave him a playful pinch. 'Huh!'

His chuckles didn't abate. After five paces he laid her on her bed and with gentle hands undid her skirt and freed her from the rest of her clothes.

'Now that we've addressed the raging inferno, let's get back to the slow burn shall, we?' He traced his hand slowly, softly down her body and unbelievably she felt the flicker all over again.

'Just for tonight.' She turned into the curve of his warm body and he lifted her to lie on top of him, his fingers gently tracing patterns down her back. She blanketed her body over his and slowly, lazily stroked him, soothing the marks she'd left on him in the passion of moments before.

Holding her head away for a moment, he smiled at her. 'Let's take it one day at a time.' Then with a simple kiss he obliterated all argument from her mind.

She woke early. Alone. She tried to block the immediate stab of pain in her heart. He'd understood then—one last night only. She doubted her ability to see out the last few weeks at Franklin's. He was far too much of a temptation and she knew he meant a whole lot more to her than just a fling. He had been right last night when he'd accused her of wanting to push him away. Of course she did because she wanted more than an affair. She wanted for ever. And that wasn't going to happen.

It had never been on the cards. He'd said six weeks was ages. Ages for their affair to burn itself out? For him maybe, but she had the sinking feeling it would take a lifetime or more for her. At least by ending it now she could start the long, slow road to recovery. Maybe she should investigate a final trip to Europe for these last few weeks. She sank deeper into the bed, for the first time ever finding the idea totally unappealing.

The key turned in the lock. She sat up, the sheet clutched to her as, round-eyed, she watched Rory stride in with several overloaded supermarket bags.

'I know what's in your pantry and, unlike you I cannot live on cereal alone.' He calmly set about stocking her tiny kitchenette with fresh coffee and a brand new stove-top caffetiere. Croissants followed, together with cheese and ham to fill them as well as raspberry jam. A couple of litres of fruit juice—one being pineapple, she noted. He was good, she had to admit it.

He tossed the Saturday paper on the bed. 'Rest up, you need it. You still look off colour.'

'How long are you planning to stay?' She finally found her voice still worked.

'At least 'til you've had something decent for breakfast. Got your energy back.' He winked outrageously.

Her cheeks burned. Her mushed-up heart started its crazy pulse again. She knew she just wasn't going to be able to help herself.

Later he dressed again, ready to leave, telling her to stay the afternoon in bed. 'I need to get home and get changed. Have dinner with me tonight. I'll cook. I'll pick you up at six. Don't forget to pack an overnight bag and bring some good walking shoes. I've got a great sightseeing trip planned for you tomorrow.'

She gaped at him. 'Last night was our one last night, Rory.'

'No. One day at a time, remember?'

Awfully, it wasn't that she couldn't say no to him; she couldn't say no to herself. Even worse was the fact that she couldn't chalk it all down to lust either. It wasn't only the sex. She liked walking with him, talking with him and, most of all, the laughing. When he smiled at her, the warmth it brought to her heart was like the most addictive drug—his company something she couldn't get enough of. Oh, yes, she'd fallen for him big style.

She thought of her mother and for once didn't think of that final heartache of what had happened with her boss. Instead she thought of her mother's love for her father. And how she'd explained it to Lissa, how she had got through the months of grief after he'd died. How she had repeated to her the old saying—'better to have loved and lost than never to have loved at all'. And she knew she couldn't give Rory up. Not even for her own well-being. Not until she was forced to.

Sunday night, after a day together that Lissa wanted to burn into her memory, he said he wanted to spend the night at her flat. She felt unsure about turning up to work together the next day.

'Well, everyone knows, Lissa—what difference is it going to make?'

None. He was right, of course. Theirs wasn't the only affair going on in the office and certainly wouldn't be the last. And he'd said himself it was one day at a time, no looking to the future. There was no future. In a few short weeks she would be flying out of the country for good.

No one batted an eyelid when they walked out of the lift together at the start of the day. And when he stopped by her desk at the end of the afternoon wanting to know what time she'd be free to go home, Gina answered for her.

And she just couldn't say no.

* * *

By Thursday they were well into a routine—a night at hers, a night at his—and Lissa felt stirrings of panic. She was merely digging a deeper hole to bury herself in at the end of this affair. Anxiety began to gnaw at her, her stomach flipping and churning, and an overwhelming tiredness started to pull her down.

'You not getting enough sleep, Lissa?' Gina asked with a coy smile as they munched on their cereal together while waiting for the computers to log on.

Lissa frowned, pushing away her cereal, her appetite lost. She knew the faint blue shadows under her eyes were darkening with each day. Frankly she felt awful, but put it down to the increasing stress she was under. Stress both caused and relieved by Rory. The best parts of her life at the moment were those spent with him. Where, without realising it, he made her forget the impending end, using either his charm and humour, or his physical skills. 'I think it's just the flu is taking longer to get over than I thought it would.'

She couldn't shake the tiredness. During the day she wanted nothing more than to curl up and snooze—she even dreamed of doing so under her desk. But at night things were different. She couldn't get enough of Rory. From the moment they walked in the door to the moment they left again the next day for work they were together, in every sense of the word.

Rory put some coffee on first thing Friday morning—he liked a hit before walking out the door. Lately he'd been having two. Lissa usually had one too, but not today. The smell was abhorrent. Nauseating. Bile rose. She left for the bathroom in a hurry, only just making it. Wiping her face down with a cold flannel after to try to stop the shaky feeling. She grimaced away the horrible taste and brushed with extra amounts of toothpaste.

'Lissa, are you OK?' He knocked on the door. No space, no let-up.

'I'm fine.' Her legs trembled. She took some deep breaths to restore calm. She stared at her pale reflection in the mirror and tried to remember what she'd eaten the day before. Could it have been the coronation chicken sandwich at lunch yesterday? That would be it.

She left the bathroom to face his intense scrutiny. He pulled upright from the wall he'd been leaning against and took her chin in his hand, tilting her face, his all-seeing eyes inspecting every aspect of her expression.

'I'm really OK.' She laughed it off, blaming the hapless sandwich.

'You shouldn't go to work.'

'I'm fine to go to work. It's all gone now, believe me!'

After another thoughtful look he relented and drove her there, her hand held in his the entire journey.

Once at work the nausea returned and unable to concentrate, she muddled about all day, barely able to cover it up. Fortunately Rory was in meetings all day. Come home time, however, he took one look at her pallor and the circles under her eyes and drove straight to his flat, abandoning the plan for drinks at the pub with the company.

Once back at his flat he bundled her into his warm, welcoming bed. She fell into it gratefully, pulling at him to join her.

He held back for a moment. 'You're still unwell.'

'I'm tired, that's all. And never too tired for this.' She ran her fingers across his jaw, feathered them down his neck and fell asleep in his arms half an hour later.

She had felt exhausted, yet at four a.m. she woke, her mind clearer and sharper than it had been for days. She remembered she'd left her toilet bag at her flat. Not too much of a problem as she now had a spare toothbrush and other items in Rory's bathroom cupboard. But that wasn't what had jolted her awake. It meant she didn't have her pill with her.

Her stomach started churning again as she lay in the darkness, listening to Rory's even breathing, feeling the weight of the arm he'd snaked around her to hold her close. It rested on her belly. And a female certainty settled in her as she listened to what her body told her. Trouble of the lifelong kind.

CHAPTER TEN

SATURDAY morning Lissa pleaded exhaustion, which was no lie, having not slept another moment since waking in the wee small hours. Reluctantly Rory agreed to them spending the night apart.

'You call me if you need me.'

She slipped to the pharmacy and within five minutes of getting in the door again she had her fears confirmed.

The blue lines appeared immediately. Not just the control line, but the line giving visual proof of what she already knew. One of the new tests so sensitive it could give a positive result even before your period was due.

She slumped on her bed. How in the hell was it possible? It wasn't possible. She hadn't missed a pill. She checked the packet to be sure—all were missing where they should be. This just couldn't be right.

His words came back to her—'one day at a time'. This was a fling with the temp who was leaving the country shortly. No strings, no commitment. Merely a wild fling for the fun of it. A 'distraction'—for him anyway. There'd probably be another temp to fill her place in a few weeks.

It wasn't serious. It never had been. It has never been meant to be anything long-term. Lissa knew this. Her mother had spelt it out clearly. Grant had proved it. Why on earth had she set herself up for this again?

Rory had said he wasn't like those guys—that there was no one else in his life. And while that was true it didn't mean he was any more serious than they had been.

What would he do? Would he walk away? Would he accuse her of trying to trap him? She told him she was on the pill and she was. It had been no lie.

She did the second test.

The nausea returned and she raced to the bathroom. She smacked her forehead with the palm of her hand in anger, raking her fingers through her hair and pulling hard on it. How could she have made this mistake? Sure, she'd been thinking about a farewell fling—but her boss? She'd known it was a dumb move but she hadn't been able to resist the lust. And now look where it had got her.

In a few weeks she would be homeless and jobless. Returning to a country in which she had no family to speak of. And to cap it all off she was pregnant.

She inhaled deeply. Her mother had survived an accidental pregnancy and done a great job of bringing her up—and that was as a teenager. At least Lissa had a few more years on her side. Shame she didn't have any more sense. Now she had gone and done the one thing her mother had warned her of. Not once but twice. The first time it had only been her job she'd lost. This time, the price was far higher.

Her thoughts returned to Rory. Terrified of his reaction, she debated when to tell him. Whether to tell him.

She blanched.

No, she had to tell him. But not yet. She couldn't face it just yet. Besides, it was so early. She should leave it a few days and retest. Maybe it was wrong. Could you get false positives?

Emotionally drained, she dragged herself back to her

bedroom and collapsed in a heap. Every old fear and doubt crowded in on her, rushing back, stronger than ever. Exhausted, she lay awake all night, lonely and at a loss.

It felt as if the next few days were a year in the passing. Each hour seemed to take for ever. She frequently went to the toilet, hoping she was wrong. Trying to hide how bad she felt from him, but unwilling to spend time apart because everything felt right again when she was in his arms. It was her sole source of comfort; weak as she was, she couldn't help herself. Despite her fears of how he would react when he found out, despite knowing their affair was going nowhere, she couldn't stay away from him. And she hated herself for it. But she couldn't fight the need, couldn't fight the fact that she just wanted to be with him for as long as she could.

And she couldn't help but recall the photos she'd seen in his album that first weekend they'd had together. The images of the emerald-eyed boy who had had such a gorgeous smile and broad shoulders even then. And she dreamed of what their own child would look like—would it be a junior Rory? Would it have those beautiful eyes? And she couldn't help but hope for yes.

But Rory was no fool. He saw how tired she was, how much of a battle it was to eat.

Finally he challenged her. 'I think you should see a doctor.'

'No!' The vehement refusal rang out.

He gave her a sharp look.

'It's just a tummy bug or something.' She winced at the pleading note in her voice.

'If it's a bug you should be over it by now. It's been more than a few days.' He was right. He knew it and she knew it.

It was impossible to mask how terrible she was feeling. Another week had passed. She'd retested. Same result.

She worried more. For the future and frantically about how she should tell Rory. She knew she had to, but she just couldn't bring herself to do it. Terrified of his reaction. Unable to bear the anger and scorn she'd certainly face. But, most of all, terrified of where this news would take them. She finally found the strength to pull away from him. She'd better get used to it after all.

She spent two nights home alone, telling him she just needed some rest and would be better in no time. She walked along her favourite riverside walks, looking at the buildings she loved, trying to recapture the excitement of being a foreigner in London and the love of life before Rory. She went to the Tate to escape into art, but only had the energy to sit and watch the people go by. And she watched them, the couples, the families, the friends, and the fear simply wouldn't go away.

The third day, after a gruelling few hours at work she left early. Back at her flat she'd just flushed away another bout of sickness when she heard the knock at the door. Only one person knocked like that. She quickly brushed her teeth and scrubbed at her face. The second she opened the door he brushed past her into the main room looking less than pleased.

'You've just been sick again, haven't you?'

She stared at him. How could he be so acute? He'd only just walked in the door.

'You look pale and your eyes are all watery.'

Definitely watery; they had been for a few days now.

'Here.' He handed her a paper bag.

'What is it?'

Sighing, he took it from her and pulled out a blue rectangular box.

Her eyes widened. A home pregnancy test.

'I think you should do it, Lissa.' He spoke softly, his expression serious.

'No.'

'Come on. I've seen my sister go through three pregnancies; I know the signs.'

Her blood turned to ice. He wasn't looking at all happy. In fact, he wasn't looking at her at all. He stared at the box he held, drumming his fingers on the top of it. All her fear came rushing to her. Every reaction she'd imagined came to her—all of them bad. Did he think she'd done it on purpose? That she'd lied to him about being on the pill? Would he hate her? Would he walk away?

'No.' She couldn't do it.

'Lissa, it'll probably be negative; you said you were on the pill. Why not take the test, just to eliminate it?'

'I don't want to.' She turned away from him, unwilling to watch the scorn she knew would flash in his face. Her hands twisted together and she tried to grow courage.

'Why not?'

She bent her head. 'I don't need to. I already know.'

His sharp inhalation spiked her adrenaline higher. 'Know what?'

She turned back to him, like the condemned refusing the blindfold, unable to resist witnessing her own execution. Her words dropped heavily between them. 'I'm pregnant.'

He stood stock-still, staring at her. She could hardly meet his gaze but was determined to, bracing herself for the explosion.

'How long have you known?' Soft, so soft it hurt more than if he'd yelled. A whisper of disbelief.

'A few days.'

'How many?' Not quite so soft now.

She coughed. 'I'm not sure; a few.'

He stared at her and she knew he saw through her, knew she'd known for a while. 'And when—' he stopped and cleared his throat '—when were you going to tell me?'

She couldn't answer that one. She didn't know.

'*Were* you going to tell me?'

'Y-yes.' Even to her own ears it sounded hesitant.

'Or not! What were you going to do—just skip the country and have my child thousands of miles away without ever telling me?' She watched as his anger grew. Knowing he was wrong but not knowing how to fix it. He stepped closer and his voice dropped. 'That's assuming you were planning to have it.'

'What? Yes, of course!' Tears, never far away, flashed in her eyes and out of defence her own anger was stoked. 'Of course I am having this baby.'

'So are you going to start taking care of yourself, then?' He swore loud and long and paced the tiny room. 'Are you going to let me in on this? Are you going to let me help you?'

He turned on his heel and dug his cell phone out of his pocket. Flicking it open, he pressed a couple of buttons. She watched him, unnerved, and wondering what on earth he was up to. His body spoke volumes. He was livid. She knotted her fingers together and waited.

'Doc? It's Rory. Sorry to bother you again…yeah…fine. Look, who's the best obstetrician you know?… OK… No chance you've got the number?… Great, got it.'

He pressed a button and, open-mouthed, Lissa, watched as he immediately punched in another number. A minute later and it appeared he'd made an appointment for her with some obstetrician for ten the next morning. His high-handedness galled her. He swung back to face her and, heedless of the storm in his eyes, she struck out at him.

'You have no right to do that. You have no right to tell me what to do.'

She had never imagined this.

He stepped up to her, speaking quickly. 'And you have no

right to keep the news of my child from me. I don't think you're in much of a position to say no right now, Lissa.'

Silently she took that one on the chin. Fair enough, and secretly she acknowledged a feeling of relief. She did want to see a doctor, talk to one. She had been feeling so awful and she wasn't sure if it was normal morning sickness or not and, after all, it wasn't as if she could ask her mother. She couldn't believe she hadn't thought of arranging it herself. She hadn't been thinking straight. She hadn't really been thinking at all.

He seemed to read her mind and his stance softened. 'You're not alone, Lissa. We're in this together.'

But that she knew to be wrong. She turned away from him. 'I'll go to the appointment.'

She sensed him also turn away to stand against the window bracing his arms against the frame, staring out across the basketball court below. 'We'll get married as soon as it can be arranged.'

'What?' She jerked her head to look at him full on.

'It shouldn't take too much to organise. Less than a couple of weeks, I think. We'll go as fast as we can.' He still stared out the window.

'What?' Her breathing came short and shallow and dizziness threatened to overcome her. She couldn't be hearing this right.

'I'm sorry it's going to be such a rush. We can always have the big party later, but we need to get legal as soon as possible.'

'Rory, I'm not going to marry you. We can't get married!' This wasn't happening. Her brain wouldn't compute. She had never expected this. Never expected him to suddenly take control of her life.

'Well, what did you think would happen? We need to get onto it; we haven't got much time.'

'Rory, we don't have to get married. I would never stop you from seeing your child.' The last thing she wanted was a

marriage forced upon him. It could only lead to unhappiness
for everybody.

He whirled to face her, his face taut. 'Your visa is close to
expiring. We need to make sure you can stay in the country.
I want this baby born in the UK.'

Oh, God.

Of course he would. Why hadn't she thought about this? Of
course he would never react as she imagined Grant would have.
Rory was a different breed entirely. But that didn't make things
right. He hadn't asked how it had happened. Hadn't challenged
her on whether she really was on the pill. Had he guessed her
feelings for him? Did he think she'd set out to trap him?

'No.' She shook her head and backed away. She hadn't
done that. She would never be so manipulative. Never use an
innocent child like that. She wouldn't use him like that. 'No.'

'Look, Lissa. I'll admit this is a hell of a shock, but the
hows and whys don't matter now. What matters is how we
deal with it and this is the only way. No child of mine is
growing up away from me.'

She felt faint. She wished she knew what he was thinking.
Wished he would blow up and reveal himself rather than
treating her as if she'd become his latest project to manage.

He stared at her grimly.

She needed space, time to think. For the first time, she truly
wanted him gone. She couldn't cope with his presence. 'Tell
me where the obstetrician is and I'll meet you there.'

'No, I'm staying here tonight.'

She didn't want him to.

And then he did reveal his thoughts. 'The fact is, I'm not
sure I can trust you, Lissa. If I hadn't forced you to admit it,
I'm not sure I would ever have known about our baby. That's
not a nice feeling.'

Sadness pulled at her. She could understand his view. He

didn't trust her and she hadn't felt able to trust him. Their blazing affair was just that, an affair, and she didn't think there was enough depth for them to be able to handle the consequences.

Rory paced across Tower Bridge on the pretext of getting a curry for dinner. He'd left Lissa, knowing she wasn't up to food. To be honest he didn't fancy it himself, but he'd needed to escape for a little bit. Part of him wanted to escape a lot, for good.

He'd just asked a woman to marry him. Hell, he hadn't exactly asked, he'd just told her it was happening. Marriage. Kids.

It had just come out of his mouth with his brain disengaged. It was what he was meant to do, the honourable thing. The only thing a decent bloke could do. Get a girl pregnant, you had to deal with it responsibly. But did he want to? Could he really live with this?

It was supposed to have been an affair. A mind-blowing affair, but an affair nonetheless. He'd always known she wasn't going to be around for long, and when she'd told him six weeks that had seemed just fine. Long enough for it to burn out. So blazing it had to be just lust.

Now the whole thing had been turned upside down completely.

It wasn't the child's fault. But he knew how damn hard work they could be. The nights of sleeplessness, the crying, the nappies. He'd seen the strain his sister had been under. Witnessed the occasional tenseness between her and her husband as they'd negotiated their way through this new development in their relationship. And they were happily married, had been university sweethearts. A love match. This was a lust match.

He walked back across the bridge again. The Tower of London was lit up and mocking him. The former prison now a tourist haven. His own heavenly tourist, Lissa, had just imprisoned him. His well-considered life plan had been beheaded. He hadn't planned for the whole serious settle-down thing to happen for a few years yet.

How the hell was it going to work? Could it work? He clenched his teeth. He'd never failed at anything he'd set his mind to. But setting his mind to this? He wasn't sure he was able to.

Lissa felt the evening pass slow and awkward. He'd come back—after an hour or so in which time she'd agonised over whether indeed he would actually return. Then she'd felt guilty all over again for doubting him when he'd walked back through the door. He'd flicked on her little telly and stared at the screen, apparently uncaring of whatever was showing and effectively ending all conversation. She crept into the bathroom to change into her pyjamas—the only time she'd worn anything in bed with Rory. After a time he switched the television off and slipped out of his clothes, silently sliding into bed but turning away from her.

For the first time they shared a bed but not each other and Lissa had never felt so alone.

CHAPTER ELEVEN

SHE woke early feeling warm and secure. Blinking, she realised Rory had curved around her in the night, his arm around her, holding her. She closed her eyes again quickly, wanting to remain in the quiet half-asleep, half-awake dreamland where the bad things could be forgotten and the blissful things could come true.

He must have been awake because he moved away from her immediately. 'Don't move. I'll get you something.'

He left the bed and soon returned with some plain toast and a glass of water. She nibbled on it. The strained silence grew.

Rory rang work for both of them explaining they'd be late. Rapidly getting used to his managerial ways, she didn't care. That was one she could let him away with.

The silence remained unbroken as he drove them to the doctor's rooms. He parked and turned to look at her as he switched off the engine.

'We'll work this out, Lissa.'

'It doesn't have to be marriage, Rory.' It couldn't be. She would be responsible for ruining his life. She could take care of herself and would manage their child. Her mother had done it, and so could she. She didn't want to be married to a man who wasn't in love with her.

Nervously she sat next to him in the waiting room. She felt appalling—had already been sick twice despite the fingers of dry toast. The doctor appeared and called for her. She stood, mortified as Rory rose as well.

He read her like a book. 'Lissa, I have touched and tasted every inch of your body. I am coming in with you.'

They walked into the consultation room together.

The doctor wasted no time getting her to do another test. She returned with it and he questioned her as they waited for the result. 'So how far along do you think you are?'

'Not very. Maybe a few weeks?'

She sat watching the test, keenly aware Rory's attention was fixed on it too. The confirming line appeared instantly.

'That's a strong positive. There's no doubt you are pregnant.'

'You can't get false positives?' She couldn't help the last vestige of hope.

He smiled and shook his head. 'Not unless you've been on fertility treatment. And you've had severe symptoms already?'

Rory answered that one, detailing her all-day sickness, the fatigue.

'I think we should do a scan. See what we can find there.'

Lissa looked up.

The doctor smiled benignly. 'Just routine. It won't take a minute—be nice to see your baby, won't it?'

She stepped behind the curtain and readied herself on the bed with the modesty blanket provided, quelling the nausea, fighting the anxiety.

The doctor pulled the curtain back and Rory came to stand by her head. Not looking away from her face, he took her hand firmly in his. A reassurance that somehow he knew she needed.

She stared up at him as fear skated through every cell. She wanted this baby to be all right regardless of what happened between her and Rory. This baby would be loved. Unplanned maybe, but certainly not unwanted.

He met her gaze squarely, somberly, his jaw tense, and again she wished she had the ability to read minds. In the past he'd been easy to read, his brilliant eyes telling her of his desire, his frustration, his humour. But now they were clouded, and she couldn't fathom his thoughts at all, let alone his feelings.

'Ah,' the doctor murmured. 'There's the problem.'

Problem. She tensed and felt Rory's hand tighten on hers. She saw the flash in his eyes, but before either could speak the doctor continued.

'Take a look at the monitor.' The doctor didn't sound concerned, he sounded kind of smug. 'There you see a heartbeat.' Lissa stared at the little blob. Kind of like a jellybean with a pulse. Fascinated, she felt her heart pull. A tiny life growing.

She hardly heard as the doctor spoke again. 'And there—' the doctor pointed across a little way on the screen '—is another.'

For a split-second Lissa stopped breathing, unwilling to understand what he meant.

'Twins.' Rory said it aloud.

'Congratulations.' The doctor beamed.

Not one, but two. Denial burst out of her.

'But I can't be pregnant; I'm on the pill!'

'It can be easy to forget one.' The doctor printed out a picture and then switched the equipment off.

'But I haven't. I didn't!'

He handed the picture to Rory, then looked at her.

'Been on any other medication recently—antibiotics?'

Her head thumped back on the pillow. Antibiotics. For her chest infection. Of course.

'You have.' The doctor smiled at her kindly as he moved to take his seat at his desk again. 'You need to use another form of protection while taking the antibiotics because they can reduce the effectiveness of the pill.'

Lissa nodded dumbly. How could she have been so dense?

Dazedly she righted her clothing before stepping out from the curtain to join the two men. As soon as she sat Rory reached out and took her hand in his. Hers shook while his was firm.

'Are there twins in the family?' The doctor tapped notes into his computer.

'Not that I'm aware of.' Not in her mother's, but she had no idea about her father's.

'Twins are increasingly common. There is some research to suggest that your chances of conceiving twins are higher if you conceive while taking the pill, and also the frequency of intercourse can be a factor.'

She couldn't look at Rory. High-frequency sex, huh? She supposed she should be grateful they weren't having triplets.

She zoned out as the doctor started talking about care for the next few months. Twins. Two babies. Double the work, double the money, *double the fun*—an imp whispered to her. It was Rory who took the information sheets he offered and Rory who asked the questions. She sat in shock. The thought of going through this alone terrified her. She thought she might just handle one; it would be hard, but if her mother had done it, then so could she. But two? At the same time? And she realised her ability to choose her future had been taken away from her. There was no choice.

She sensed the appointment was concluding when she heard Rory quietly ask another question.

'Can we still…uh…?' His voice trailed away. 'I don't want to hurt her, or them.'

The specialist obviously understood the silent bit in the middle. 'Intimate relations won't do anybody any harm, but you might need to get creative a few months down the track because she's going to be very round with this pregnancy.'

He still wanted to have sex with her? He was still interested? Despite the shock and stress a flicker of pleasure surged. She still wanted him too, but the situation had just taken an even more dramatic turn and there was more to a relationship than sex. Even the most amazing sex didn't make a marriage work.

She paid no attention as the next appointment was booked and was quite unaware of how they ended up walking along the footpath back to the car.

Rory breathed in deeply, needing an extra dose of oxygen to help clear his head. Twins. He couldn't believe it. He hadn't wanted to believe she was pregnant at all, not logically—he didn't see how it was possible. But he'd had a feeling in his bones. Was there such a thing as male intuition?

The antibiotics. It felt good to have that explained. He hadn't doubted Lissa, had believed her when she'd said she was on the pill. Figured maybe she'd forgotten it once. Hell, he hadn't really thought about it at all. He was still trying to get his head around the whole idea.

And now there were two.

Double the amount of nappies and noise and half the amount of sleep as one baby. It didn't bear thinking about.

He glanced at her. She was staring down at the footpath, her hand lax in his, not holding him, but not pulling away either.

'Talk to me,' he said.

'I can't believe you asked that.'

'What?' He couldn't stop the wry grin. 'About whether we can still sleep together?'

She nodded.

'Lissa, I fully intend to have sex with my wife. Lots of sex.'

My wife. The words seemed to gum up his mouth and he froze. He let go of her hand to run his fingers through his hair and hoped his doubt was masked from her. He'd once told her he wouldn't hurt her and he didn't want to, but he couldn't be sure he loved her. He couldn't be sure he could cope with any of this.

'I've an idea,' she said softly. 'I don't think we should make any big decisions yet. Why don't we just take it one day at a time?'

He blew out a huff of air in relief. He looked at her, wondering if she was as doubt-plagued as him. Of course she was. They needed space to think, to see if there was another solution. One day at a time. Trouble was, there weren't that many days left.

It should have been one of the most exciting weekends of her life. On a plane with a gang of friends from work, off to enjoy an all-expenses-paid weekend in a beautiful city with one of the most incredible buildings in the world to admire—and it housed great works of art. Bliss, right?

The nausea on the plane was only just manageable. She told the others she often suffered from air sickness and it enabled her to sneak to her hotel room early and not go clubbing with the rest of them. Despite the exhaustion she couldn't sleep. The dilemma and doubts raced in her mind. And she missed Rory. Missed the warmth of him, the comfort in his arms despite the chasm that lay between them during the day.

She decided to forgo the shopping trip and head straight to the Guggenheim. Wanting to see it in the bright morning light as well as lit up at the function scheduled for that night.

She walked around marvelling at the curves, the genius melding of glass, stone and titanium. Her digital camera hung uselessly from her wrist; pointless even trying to capture the magnificence and complexity in thirty-five millimetres. As she stared up at the skyline her vision began to wobble. She blinked rapidly to clear it but the dizziness only increased, and then the pain came, knifing into her, and as the blackness swallowed her sight she could only call for one thing. Rory.

It was the longest five hours of his life. He wished he could break into the pilots' cabin and demand they put their foot down, or make the wind blow them there faster or something, anything.

He'd never forget that phone call. The terror, the difficulty in getting air to his lungs. The shock at the realisation that he'd been on the verge of losing the most precious thing in his life.

They'd told him he didn't need to fly over, that they'd get her home OK. But that wasn't OK for him. He needed to see her, needed to be with her, needed *her* full stop. Nothing else mattered.

In the end the woman next to him insisted he take the aisle seat—she obviously couldn't cope with his fidgeting. He went and stood by the emergency exit, pacing in two square feet for the rest of the flight.

He'd so nearly stuffed up. He'd been umming and ahhing when he should have been moving heaven and earth to ensure he got what he wanted.

Lissa. Whole, healthy, his.

How could he have been so uncertain? He couldn't believe it had taken this to make him understand what he wanted. He'd been increasingly anxious; the panic over her looming departure and their situation had rendered him unable to think, unable to see his way through. Now it all came with brilliant clarity. He had been such an idiot. He'd just had the biggest fright of his life and he wasn't chancing it happening again.

She lay on the hotel bed, pale but calm. He fought to maintain an equally calm exterior, but his insides churned.

'It's OK Rory. I'm OK.'

He'd obviously failed to hide his alarm. 'You don't look OK.'

'Just tired, that's all. The doctor said I have to take it easy.'

He knew this. He'd spoken to the doctor just before entering her room. She was exhausted, her body firing a warning shot. Telling her she needed to take things easy. Minimum stress, maximum TLC and she and the babies would be just fine. He nearly maxed out with guilt. The sense of responsibility was huge, and his need to protect her primal.

There was only one way he could ensure it. His gut had spoken for him when he'd first found out she was pregnant. The solution simple. But his brain had interfered and pulled him back, letting doubt in instead of going with the base emotion. Love.

Now he needed to convince her it was the only thing to do. Marriage, a.s.a.p. And the way to get her to agree was by using the babies and her looming departure as the bargaining chips. He'd make her see the sense of it. He needed to make it OK. It was a huge step, but it was the only one they had. The only one he finally realised he wanted to take.

She looked away from him, out the tiny plane window from which nothing could be seen but the dark night sky. Her pale face was reflected and, despite her physical weakness, he read the determination there.

'I'm sorry I didn't tell you sooner about the pregnancy, but I promise I was going to. I just didn't know when or how. I was scared.'

'Scared of what?' He studied her. Her cheeks were rosier now and she still wouldn't meet his eye. 'What did you think I'd do?'

His heart sank. 'You thought I'd walk away, didn't you? That I'd abandon you.'

She looked around at that and made to speak, but he waved her silent. He could read the look in her eyes and knew she had doubted him. 'When have I ever given you reason not to trust me?'

'It wasn't you. It was the whole…whole situation.'

Sure, the situation was difficult, but the fact was she didn't trust him. He was nothing like her ex-boyfriend, but that didn't matter. She still didn't believe in him. He hadn't got anywhere with her. It hurt more than he cared to consider. Without trust, how could there be love?

He knew things had happened faster for him than they had for her. He'd fallen for her. He kicked himself for not recognising it sooner. Couldn't believe it had been the thought of nearly losing her completely that had jerked the fact into his consciousness. Events had overtaken him.

But he didn't know if she loved him. Yes, she wanted him; yes, they were compatible on many levels other than the obvious, but did she actually love him or was this merely a hot affair? He had to try regardless.

'Lissa, I want to marry you. We can make this work. It's the only way forward. I can take care of you and the babies. You have to let me.' It was the nearest he could come right now to a declaration. He knew she wasn't ready for him to swear undying love. She wouldn't believe him. Another difficult situation, more bad timing. And frankly he wasn't ready to put himself on the line like that. Not when he really hadn't any idea where her heart lay.

'OK.'

His breath hissed out. His gums were sore from clenching his teeth together so tightly. He'd been so uncertain of her answer. Been so ready to present his case, working through the arguments the entire journey to get her.

But she'd agreed, just like that. Not that she looked that

happy about it. He kept himself in check, not reaching for her and loving her as he wanted.

Well, if she didn't love him yet, she would. He would do everything in his power to make it happen. He loved her. She was his and carrying his two children. But he didn't want to scare her off with flowery vows. It was early, early days. No, the way forward was to get the ring on her finger first, and then show her. Once they were married he'd prove to her it was the only thing their hearts would let them do.

Until finding out about the twins she'd refused to contemplate a wedding. He remembered what she'd said at lunch with James and Marnie. She'd said she would only ever marry for love. And that was the problem. She didn't love him. Only now she was backed into a corner. He felt desperately sorry for her. Wanted to scoop her up, protect her, tell her it would all be all right, tell her how much he loved her. But he forced it all to stay inside. He couldn't tell her. Not yet.

She finished at Franklin. He worried about her, alone and isolated in his flat. She'd chatted briefly on the phone to Gina but had told her nothing. He wouldn't have minded if she had—they were all going to find out soon enough and he figured she might need her friend right now. But instead she'd spent the time soothing Gina over some falling-out with her friend Karl.

In only a few days he watched, helpless, as she withdrew. She allowed him to make the decisions with seemingly little interest in what he was deciding, signed the visa application forms without even reading them. Her fatigue worried him, the difficulty she had in finding something to tempt her to eat. Sure, the pregnancy was knocking her around, but he knew it was more than that. He didn't know how to combat her unhappiness.

But in the night when he slid into bed with her, she turned

to him, time and time again. In the darkness, or the semi-light of dawn, she wrapped her legs around him as they came together, the difficulties forgotten in the moments of physical closeness and relief. In those moments he felt she was loving him and he wanted that more than anything.

He looked down at her and saw her eyes were closed. He hated that. Usually she gazed right at him. Made him feel that she was drinking him in with her eyes as well as her body. Letting him see into her warm, generous soul. But now he felt shut out.

He pulled almost right out of her. 'Open your eyes.'

They flicked open, and slowly he re-entered her, gradually plunging as deeply as he could. Holding her gaze, he pulled out again. Intently he watched her as he continued the slow, exquisite torture of being almost all the way out and then all the way in. Emphasising the purpose of them joining, making her see it was him there with her, inside her, longing to be part of her. That they were right *together*, that they were meant to be.

Her eyes widened further, her reddened mouth parted and her hips rose to meet him, to hurry him. He wasn't having it, not yet.

Bending his head, he kissed her with all the intensity and love he felt. He tasted her cry of ecstasy and held her as she trembled, only then willing to release himself.

When he lifted his head to look at her he saw her eyes were closed again. And he couldn't help the feeling that, somehow, he'd lost her.

CHAPTER TWELVE

EXHAUSTED Lissa sat on top of her old pack and tried for what felt like the fiftieth time to pull the zip closed. She'd boxed the books and clothes she no longer wanted and left a sign on them to be taken to the charity store. All she had left was the travel backpack she'd left New Zealand with, a suit bag and her small daypack. She'd come to the flat the instant Rory had left for work and nearly killed herself with the effort of getting it shipshape. They were supposed to be moving her gear from the flat and she would be living with Rory permanently. Things had happened so fast and she couldn't keep up the pretence any more.

This weekend she would be meeting Rory's family for the first time. What a way to be introduced. Here's the girl I got pregnant and now we're having a shotgun wedding. She couldn't bear it.

She had tried to argue they needn't marry in a hurry, but he insisted. Rory the honourable, trapped into a wedding, a lifelong sentence. She had been so wrong to doubt him earlier. He was nothing like Grant. He had integrity, always one to 'do the right thing'.

Oh, sure, he wanted her. The sexual attraction between them was dynamite, but it wasn't enough. It couldn't last, es-

pecially under the strain of having not one, but two newborn
babies to look after.

At least he hadn't pretended to her. He hadn't used those three
little words. He wouldn't. Lying for Rory was impossible. He'd
told her once he was an honest person and so he was. Painfully
so, Lissa now acknowledged. She would have believed him if
he'd said them, simply because she longed for it so much. But
they were unsaid. Unsaid because they were unfelt.

I love you.

Rory. And she did. Wholly. And it wasn't the hormones
from her pregnancy driving her towards security; she'd known
she was sunk since that first weekend they'd had together. For
her it wasn't just the fire of passion, it was the warmth of
humour, the sunny pleasure of common interests, the glow she
felt by spending time with him.

She loved him and hated the idea of him stuck in a one-
sided marriage. Couldn't cope with the thought of him
unhappy, saddled with a wife he hadn't wanted, unable to be
free to find a woman he would love in the intense, all-con-
suming way she loved him.

One day at a time. Their affair had been on the countdown
to its end and not once had he brought up any suggestion of
a future. He hadn't planned on there being one. It should have
been over and she couldn't bear knowing their marriage was
because it had to be, not because he wanted it. That was why
she had to do it. She had to leave.

With superhuman effort she lugged her bags downstairs
and to the street where she stood waiting for a cab to go past.

Heathrow Terminal Three was as busy as ever with people
arriving and departing everywhere. She held tightly to the little
bag in which she kept her passport and the ticket she'd booked
months ago. One way to Auckland, New Zealand. She handed

over the millions to the cabbie who had driven her the long drive there. He must have sensed her exhaustion and despair because he was out of the cab and loading her bags onto a trolley for her before she had the chance to ask him.

She headed slowly towards the Air New Zealand counters, already hearing the familiar accent from the people in the queue. She pushed the heavy trolley into place at the back of the queue and dug out the ticket to check her flight number.

'Daddy!'

The little boy careered through the snaking line of people, narrowly missing her trolley, and threw himself at the legs of the man who must be his father. The man in question bent down and, with a grin as wide as the little boy's arms had been, scooped him up and swung him around. The child's chortles were the sweetest sound. His father hugged him close and both were beaming as they embraced.

Daddy.

Her hand crept to her belly. And her brain started working again with clarity. How could she deprive her children of knowing their father? A father who might not be in love with their mother, but who certainly wanted them. A father who would love and protect them. She had no right to do that. Especially when she knew how it felt to want a dad so much. She'd dreamed of meeting him, spent years wondering what he must have been like, what his family were like, wishing like crazy fate hadn't been so cruel as to take him from both her and her mother.

She'd felt bitter envy of her classmates on sports days and festivals when both parents had turned up to take pride in their achievements. A father to scoop a wee girl up and swing her around. How she would have loved that.

Her children would never forgive her if they'd had that opportunity and she'd denied them it. Aside from herself and her own love for them, she had nothing else to offer them—no aunts or uncles, no grandparents, not even the basics: a job, or a house for herself. Rory could give them all that. How could she be so negligent? How could she be so selfish? She bowed her head. There was a way around this, she just had to be strong.

Blinking back tears, she took the ticket in both hands and, before she could think further, she tore it in two. She looked around for a rubbish bin—damn, they never had them. With a piece of the ticket in each hand she pulled the trolley around and headed back towards the exit and the rank of cabs. And there stood Rory.

Just inside the door, watching her from a distance. Tall, pale and grim and angrier than she'd ever imagined he could be.

She didn't take her eyes off him as she moved towards him, saw him take a deep breath as he strode towards her. 'What the hell do you think you're doing?' His voice carried across the terminal. 'You're not going. Not going anywhere.'

'I know. I'm not. I'm not going.' She spoke quickly. To prove it she held out her hands, offering him the torn ticket. He took the pieces, one in each hand, looking down as he held them together, reading the destination. The hardness in his jaw failed to ease even a smidgeon. His hands curled into fists, screwing up the ticket halves as he thrust them into his pockets and glared at her.

'How did you know I was here?' She wished he hadn't caught her. She didn't want him to know about her cowardice.

'I tried calling you at home. Got concerned when you didn't answer. Then I remembered this was the day you were originally scheduled to fly.' The fury poured off him and she could sense hurt in his expression as well.

Utterly remorseful, she made to head for the exit. With a growl he motioned her aside so he could push the trolley. She hurried alongside him as they went to the cab at the head of the queue, slid into the seat as he stowed her bag, and braced herself. As soon as he'd given instructions to the cabbie she turned to him, the words spouting forth, wanting to make things as right as they could be.

'I'm sorry I put you through this. You've been nothing but wonderful to me, Rory, and you didn't deserve this.'

His tense position didn't alter; if anything he grew even more rigid. She forced herself to continue.

'I will marry you, Rory, if you still think it's best. But you have to promise me something.'

His eyes sparked and she sensed he was only just reining himself in.

She looked away, twisting her hands together. 'We've been having an affair and, now, things have become complicated. But I don't want your life ruined because of one simple mistake. If you meet someone, fall in love with someone, then I'll just bow out; we can have a quiet divorce. I'm sure…' her voice caught '…sure we can arrange something for the children. They need you and your family. I don't want to trap you in a loveless marriage.'

She chanced a look back at him.

He was even paler than when she'd first seen him at the airport. 'Loveless marriage?'

'I know you don't love me, Rory. And that's OK, really it is. I don't expect you to. It's not possible.'

'Not possible?'

She felt her flush mount, her skin felt clammy. 'Everything has been so sudden.'

There was a pause.

'You don't think it's possible to fall in love with someone quickly?'

She looked at him, fear stabbing—had he guessed? How humiliating.

'Isn't it possible to fall in love almost the moment you meet?' He paused and took an audible breath.

Tears welled and she looked away from him. 'It's possible,' she mumbled. Of course it was; she knew first hand.

'It's possible all right. Especially if she's a tall, willowy type with big brown eyes and hair like golden honey.' The words came out angrily, as if they were being forced out.

She turned to look at him as she registered the repetition of how he'd described her that first night. She hadn't forgotten and now she knew he hadn't either. He was still pale, still tense; his eyes flashed a message she was terrified of believing.

'It's possible.' The heat in her cheeks became unbearable. Her heart thumped so hard she thought it might burst from her body. But she took her courage in both hands and in 'Especially if he had wickedly gleaming green eyes and a smile high-wattage enough to melt the Antarctic.'

The tension broke to a tentative dawn. He leaned a little closer, the vestige of one of those smiles playing at the corners of his full mouth. 'Are you going to lay your cards on the table, Lissa?'

'I thought I'd let you go first,' she whispered, unable to stop leaning towards him too, unable to stop the hope burgeoning in her heart, breathing deeply for the first time in days.

He spoke quickly, intently. 'I can't go falling in love with someone else, Lissa, because I only have one heart and it's already been taken.' He reached out and took her chin in his hand, the touch light and yet it kicked her desire level sky-high.

'I fell in love with you the minute I saw you stepping out onto the balcony that night. I couldn't stop myself following you, wanting to meet you, find out about you. At first I put it down to sheer lust, but I was deluding myself. It's always been more.' He inched closer. 'I love you.'

He drew her closer still, so their lips were almost touching.

'I love you too, Rory.' The admission whispered out just as he moved to close the gap entirely.

He pulled back instantly. 'Say that again.'

'I love you.'

He gripped her upper arms, squeezing as if checking she really was there. 'Thank God.' And then he kissed her. Tiny kisses over and over, all over until she begged him to kiss her properly. And when he did she felt sure she'd died and gone to heaven.

'We have a lot of talking to do,' he muttered before claiming her mouth again.

None of it got done in the cab. The rest of the ride back to his flat was spent indulging in lush kisses that soothed and ⬛⬛⬛⬛ the same time.

He made her wait while he quickly lugged her bags inside. She could hardly contain her excitement, didn't want him disappearing from view for even those few seconds. Returning to her, he took her hand as she stepped out and then swung her into his arms.

'No more snowboard-style?' she teased.

'Hell, no!' He laughed. 'At least, not for about eight months or so. Besides, I'm practising.'

'What for?'

'The whole over-the-threshold thing.'

He carried her indoors, marching straight to his bedroom.

'I thought you might need a lie-down.'

'Oh, absolutely.'

He stood her on her feet, but still cradled her to him, his hand sweeping down her back in long strokes. She flared, wanting to be with him, wanting to make love.

Then his stomach rumbled.

She giggled.

'I didn't have lunch.' He grinned back ruefully.

'So what do you fancy, then?' she asked.

His smile was immediate and broad. 'Well,' he said, musing slowly, 'I thought I'd have this for starters.' He traced his finger around her lips, pulling the lower one down a little and brushing the inside. A ripple of excitement went through her. He lifted his finger from her lips and she licked them in anticipation.

'Then,' he continued softly, not taking his eyes from hers, 'I thought I'd have these for main.' He took one breast in each hand and with his thumbs stroked slightly. She was sure he was able to feel the taut nipples through her sweatshirt. She smiled, liking the idea so far.

'And then—' he was smiling with a devilish glint now '—I thought I'd have this for dessert.' He slid a hand down and brazenly rubbed across her belly and curved into her pelvis.

She sucked in a deep breath and wantonly squeezed her thighs together, effectively trapping his hand.

'Thing is,' he said with a small helpless gesture and an innocent look, 'sometimes I just have to have dessert first.'

She reflected desire back at him. Suddenly all patience was lost. They kissed and kissed again, her passion and happiness effervescent, sparking. She twisted against him, wanting to drive him as crazy as he did her.

'There's only one thing in the world I want more than you in my arms right now,' he said, his voice sounding rough.

'What's that?' she asked breathlessly.

'You *naked* in my arms right now.'

'I think that can be arranged.'

'I was hoping you might say that.'

Action was instantaneous. She pulled her sweatshirt and tee shirt over her head at the same time and stood just in bra and jeans. He yanked his tie off before taking over immediately, reaching for her, ravishing her. She fought with the buttons on his shirt, undoing them and slipping it off together with his jacket. He was gorgeous. Their lips remained locked while they hastily undid belt buckles and buttons and tried to kick off jeans and trousers.

He laughed hungrily. 'Shoes, darling. Shoes.' He bent and slipped off hers before hurriedly attending to his own. He couldn't move fast enough for her. She needed to hold him close. Finally freed from their clothing, they literally fell onto her bed in a tangle of limbs. He held her firmly, using his mouth to explore every inch of her. She fought his grip as she tried to do the same to him. It was frantic and passionate, both desperate for fulfilment.

'I can't get enough of you,' she confessed feverishly as she pressed kisses across his chest. He was driving her wild. She wanted everything, all of it right now, but at the same time she wanted to savour it, cherish every moment. The dilemma was driving her crazy.

'It's OK, beautiful.' He shushed her with a deep kiss. 'We have for ever.' The kiss sealed them and their rhythms matched. He was right. He was her lifelong mate and this was the first dance of many more to come. They teased each other until, unable to wait any longer, he settled his weight over her and she sighed with contentment as he pushed inside. She would never have enough of this.

She lifted a hand to frame his face as they both stilled to savour the moment. 'I love you.'

His mouth moved over hers—a tender torment as his body began a slow and welcome rhythm. 'You're everything to me.'

He gathered her closer and together they moved slowly at first, and then with increasing ferocity until they were both past the point of tolerance and with joyous cries they tumbled together from the heights.

Lying twisted, still connected, panting, she had to ask. 'I

can't believe you love me. Are you sure? It's not just because of the babies?'

He gathered a section of her hair and pulled on it teasingly. 'Silly. I'm excited about the babies, of course I am. But it's you I love, Lissa. I can't even imagine them yet. It's you I want. You I don't want to live without.'

'But why didn't you tell me?'

'How could I? I really wasn't sure where I stood with you, Lissa. I didn't want to freak you out and send you running by declaring undying love for you when you were still learning you could trust me. I didn't want to overwhelm you.'

Her eyes smarted. She had been such an idiot. Letting her fears and insecurities from her past colour her judgment of him. She'd almost walked away from the best thing ever to happen in her life. Rory. OK, so it hadn't exactly been slow and steady as she'd once thought she wanted. It had been fast and furious and much, much better.

'Don't cry, beautiful, please don't cry.' He tilted her head back so he could see into her eyes.

'Happy tears.'

'Oh. Well. That's OK, then.'

They lay close again. She felt complete and relaxed until another thought needled into her mind.

'Rory, what are your family going to say?' Terrified about meeting them, she waited anxiously for his answer.

His smile turned wicked. 'They can't wait to meet you. My sister's been hounding me for ages.'

'Ages? She's known about me for ages?' She sat up and looked down at his amused expression.

He nodded. 'I had to return her car to her that first night, remember? She took one look at my face and knew something was up. Immediately guessed it was a woman, and has been crowing to my mother since that she knew first.'

'What about the babies? Will they mind about that?'

He really laughed that time. 'Hell, no, they'll be thrilled. Mum has been nagging me for some time about settling down, having a family, not wasting all my energy on my career. I'm pushing thirty, you know.' He said it in such a way she knew he was mimicking his mother and she laughed.

He ran his hand over her belly, his eyes softening. 'They won't be too much younger than their cousins; heaven help they won't be influenced too badly by those toads.'

Lissa's smile broadened, the doting uncle all too apparent.

'They'll love you, Lissa, don't worry about that.'

Suddenly he sat up. 'There's something I need to do. Something I need to rectify.'

She waited while he reached down the side of the bed and scrabbled for his trousers. Her heart thudded as he pulled out a small black velvet box from the pocket.

He looked up with an intent expression.

Emotion threatened to overwhelm her. 'You don't need to do this Rory.'

'I do.' He smiled at her. 'I do.'

Her eyes filled again. Damn hormones.

'What am I going to say when our kids ask about our marriage? That I just said to you, "Right, that's it, we're getting married." You deserve a proposal, Lissa. You deserve to be asked properly.' He paused, a humorous light in his eye. 'Just make sure you give the right answer.'

She smiled away the tears. 'And what am I going to say to the kids when they ask where this beautiful proposal took place? Not some fancy restaurant, or some scenic mountain-top. But in bed with your father, both naked in the middle of the afternoon?'

He shrugged. 'Beautiful things happen in bed with you, Lissa.'

He knelt in front of her, his light-hearted look replaced with a sincerity she felt in her soul. 'Lissa, I love you and will to my dying day. Will you marry me?'

'Yes, I will, Rory, because I love you too.'

He opened the box and held it out to her. 'I know lots of people go to choose a ring together, but I saw this and knew it was right.'

Not right, perfect. The ring was beautiful. A large brilliant cut diamond flanked on either side by two golden topaz. All three stones glittered.

'They remind me of your eyes, the golden lights in them and your hair. There are two, one for each baby. But the diamond is you, Lissa. You're the prize for me.'

The tears flowed again as he lifted it from the box and slid it down her finger, home.

'You really thought about this.'

His smile was one of the sort that really knocked her sideways. 'Like I said, it was right.'

'It is. When did you get it?'

'I picked it up this morning, I knew it couldn't wait any longer; I needed to tell you how I was feeling. I knew you were unhappy and it was my last shot.'

'And then you came and found me headed to the airport.' She felt terrible.

His smile vanished. 'Yeah, that was a real low point.'

'I'm sorry. I could never have done it, you know. I thought I could, but I just couldn't.' She took his face in her hands, smoothing away the grim recollection.

He bent his head, kissing her with such loving tenderness the tears in her eyes spilled over. He kissed them away gently. Her heart felt complete. He lifted her onto his lap and she pushed closer to him, onto him, and together they increased the rhythm, creating the most exquisite friction. Passion overrode the tender tranquillity and they clung to each other with quickened breathing. At last she knew the joy of loving and being loved. Wholly. Elation soared through her.

Some time later he spoke again. 'There is one other thing I have to tell you.'

She raised her brows; he sounded guilty.

'I've booked the honeymoon.'

'You have?'

He nodded decisively. 'Florence. I promised you I'd take you—remember?'

How could she forget the magic night she'd met him? 'Ponte Vecchio.'

'And gelato for my beautiful Venus.' He lifted his head off the pillow. 'Can you have gelato when pregnant?'

'I can't think why not.'

'What flavour are you going to have?'

'Lemon.'

'Really? I thought it would have been raspberry.'

She shook her head. 'Definitely lemon. I love the smell of lemon. But maybe—' she twinkled '—maybe I'll have a scoop of each.'

'Two, huh?'

'Double the pleasure.'

'Always.'

And it would be, always with him.

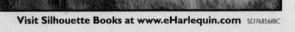

HARLEQUIN *Presents*®

**Harlequin Presents would like
to introduce brand-new author**

Christina Hollis

and her fabulous debut novel—

ONE NIGHT IN HIS BED!

Sienna, penniless and widowed, has caught the eye
of the one man who can save her—Italian tycoon
Garett Lazlo. But Sienna must give herself to him
totally, for one night of unsurpassable passion....

Book #2706

*Look out for more titles by Christina, coming soon—
only from Harlequin Presents!*

◆ HARLEQUIN®

Mediterranean
NIGHTS™

*Sometimes you need someone to teach you the
things you already know....*

Coming in February 2008

CABIN
FEVER

by
Mary Leo

Vacationing aboard *Alexandra's Dream* with her
two kids and her demanding mother-in-law,
widow Becky Montgomery is not about to start
exploring love again. But when she meets Dylan
Langstaff, the ship's diving instructor, she realizes
she might be ready to take the plunge....

Available wherever books are sold
starting the second week of February.

QUEENS *of* R♥MANCE

The world's favorite romance writers

New and original novels you'll treasure forever from internationally bestselling Presents authors, such as:

Lynne Graham

Lucy Monroe

Penny Jordan

Miranda Lee

and many more.

Don't miss

THE GUARDIAN'S FORBIDDEN MISTRESS

by Miranda Lee

Book #2701

Look out for more titles from your favorite Queens of Romance, coming soon!

HARLEQUIN® *Presents*®

THE ROYAL HOUSE OF NIROLI

Always passionate, always proud.

**The richest royal family in the world—
a family united by blood and passion,
torn apart by deceit and desire.**

By royal decree Harlequin Presents is delighted to bring you
The Royal House of Niroli. Step into the glamorous, enticing
world of the Nirolian Royal Family. As the king ails he must
find an heir.... Each month an exciting new installment
follows the epic search for the true Nirolian king. Eight heirs,
eight passionate romances, eight fantastic stories!

A ROYAL BRIDE
AT THE SHEIKH'S
COMMAND
by Penny Jordan
Book #2699

A desert prince makes his claim to the
Niroli crown.... But to Natalia Carini
Sheikh Kadir is an invader—he's already
taken Niroli, now he's demanding her
as his bride!

HARLEQUIN *Presents*

The Rich, the Ruthless and the Really Handsome

How far will they go to win their wives?

A trilogy by Lynne Graham

Prince Rashad of Bakhar, heir to a desert kingdom;
Leonidas Pallis, scion of one of Greece's leading dynasties
and Sergio Torrente, an impossibly charismatic,
self-made Italian billionaire.

Three men blessed with power, wealth and looks—
what more can they need? Wives, that's what...and
they'll use whatever means to get them!

THE GREEK TYCOON'S DEFIANT BRIDE
by Lynne Graham
Book #2700

Maribel was a shy virgin when she was bedded by impossibly
handsome Greek tycoon Leonidas Pallis. But when Maribel
conceives his child, Leonidas will claim her...as his bride!

**Don't miss the final installment of Lynne Graham's
dazzling trilogy! Available next month:**

THE ITALIAN BILLIONAIRE'S
PREGNANT BRIDE
Book #2707
www.eHarlequin.com

HP12700